A King Production presents…

D1593175

Stackin'
PAPER
VII

Who Want
Smoke…

A Novel

JOY DEJA KING

Cover concept by Joy Deja King
Cover Model: Joy Deja King

Graphic design: www.anitaart79.wixsite.com/bookdesign
Typesetting: Anita J.

Library of Congress Cataloging-in-Publication Data;
King, Deja Joy
Stackin' Paper Part 7: a novel/by Joy Deja King
For complete Library of Congress Copyright info visit;
www.joydejaking.com Twitter: @joydejaking

A King Production
P.O. Box 912, Collierville, TN 38027

A King Production and the above portrayal logo are trademarks of A King Production LLC

This Book is Dedicated To My:

Family, Readers and Supporters.
I LOVE you guys so much. Please believe that!!

-

A special THANK YOU to RG, for motivating me
to get back to doing what I love.
I will always adore you.
For Life.

—Joy Deja King

"You Could Send Your Best Man,
You Gon' Lose Your Best Hitter..."

~Who Want Smoke??~

A KING PRODUCTION
Stackin'
PAPER
VII
Who Want
Smoke...
A Novel
JOY DEJA KING

Chapter One

War

Genesis listened intently to the pastor, who was reading scriptures aloud at the christening ceremony for his firstborn and only grandchild. The message penetrated his soul and Genesis prayed his grandson would grow up to understand he must trust in God's love for him. As he continued to cling onto every word, one scripture struck a chord that sent chills down Genesis' spine.

"It says in Acts 2:38, Repent and be baptized, every one of you, in the name of Jesus Christ for the forgiveness of your sins. And you will receive the gift of the Holy Spirit." The pastor seemed to be speaking directly to Genesis and he embraced it. After the pastor's sermon, it was followed by prayers and hymns. Genesis stood and watched proudly as Desi was immersed in water and the pastor stated, "I baptize you in the name of the Father, and of the Son, and of the Holy Spirit."

"This was such a beautiful ceremony," Talisa turned to her husband and said.

"Yes, it was," Genesis nodded. He felt the ceremony symbolized spiritual cleansing and rebirth for not only his grandson but possibly for him too. "We should head over to the venue where the reception is being held, try to beat the crowd," Genesis suggested.

"Sure, but do I have time to speak with someone for a second?" Talisa asked.

"Of course. I'll go have the driver pull the car up front. I'll see you shortly," Genesis said, giving his wife a kiss.

"I won't be long." Talisa smiled before hurrying off.

Genesis headed out the church, and when he opened the door, clear skies and the bright afternoon sun welcomed him. He inhaled the fresh air, feeling blessed that he witnessed the christening of his grandson and was alive to see another day.

As Genesis stood on top of the stairs, taking in the serene surroundings, his peacefulness was disrupted by the unmistakable sound of a barrage of bullets.

The shootout began when a gunman on a motorcycle tried to break through the security cordon set up outside the church. The assailant was carrying an explosive device. While security exchanged shots with the man on the motorcycle, a dark Chrysler 300 sped west. Genesis' driver promptly jumped out the SUV exchanging gunfire with the men in the car. The vehicle turned north, and gunshots continued to be fired at Genesis and inadvertently at the christening attendees, as they were now exiting the church. The vehicle crashed midway down the block, and those inside the vehicle fled on foot.

Many were still inside the church making small talk when the violence broke out. It sounded like an onslaught of bombs were ignited, and immediately the gates were closed. Other passersby were running, taking cover from the gunfire in a nearby restaurant. Everyone stayed inside until the shower storm of bullets ceased. Once people were able to leave, they stepped outside and were shocked to see blood covering every inch of the concrete. You could hear screams as most were inconsolable and overwhelmed with grief.

The shootout outside the church killed a total of six people including a police officer. A young child was also wounded in the gunfire exchange, with some bullets penetrating the surrounding buildings and homes.

The first assailant who was riding the motorcycle, was lying dead on the ground with his brains blown out and his face covered in blood. The other gunmen used AR-15 style semiautomatic rifles in the tragic attack, as the shooters were prepared to wreak havoc. They fired indiscriminately, making everyone a target and without regard to the sanctity of life. Innocent bystanders became casualties of the gunfire. The level of brazenness sent the normally quiet street into chaos.

When Talisa ran out the church searching for Genesis, she stepped directly into the chaos. The once clear sunny skies shifted to clouds, darkness and rain. There were puddles of blood in every direction, and one led Talisa directly to her husband.

"Genesis!" Talisa let out an ear-piercing scream and she fell to her knees. There was a crowd gathered around him, but Genesis didn't say a word. He wasn't coherent, so Talisa just held on to his still bloodied body, praying over him.

Genesis was staring up at the dark sky, "I love you," he mustered up enough strength to say before taking his very last breath.

Genesis suddenly raised up in bed with heavy, rapid breathing.

"Baby, are you okay?" Talisa turned to Genesis who was sitting up, drenched in sweat and his chest pounding.

"No, I'm not okay," he exhaled forcefully. "You and Genevieve are leaving first thing after the homegoing reception for Nico."

"What are you talking about...where are we going?"

"I don't know yet. I'll make the decision once you're both on the jet."

"You're not coming with us?" Talisa questioned.

"I have to stay here."

"Then let us stay here with you," she said, placing her hand on Genesis' shoulder.

"I'm at war. It's not safe for you to be here. You and Genevieve need to go. I won't make the same mistake twice."

"Genesis, what mistake are you talking

5

about?" Talisa stared at her husband with confusion.

"You remember what happened last time I went to war. I watched you die. You couldn't raise our son because that sick sonofabitch held you as a prisoner on an island. I wish I could bring Arnez back to life just so I can kill that muthafucka again," Genesis seethed.

"Baby, Arnez is dead and I'm here with you now."

"And I plan to keep it that way. I'll do whatever it takes to protect you and Genevieve. The only blood on my hands will be Maverick's," Genesis promised.

Chapter Two

Never Say Goodbye

Aaliyah and Angel glanced up at the fresh floral chandelier hanging from the ceiling when they entered the waterfront French Chateau in the Hamptons. They walked towards the open doors that led to a beautifully draped tent, with a covered structure, that created an intimate space. It allowed for an outdoor reception, but the sides of the tent were left open to allow for a scenic view of the tranquil property. The cascading drapery created softness and an inviting entry. There was a custom ordered tree placed in the center, which held hundreds of candles. It was the centerpiece for cherished photographs of Nico with his loved ones.

"Aaliyah, I'm glad you're finally here. It's wonderful to see you." A sense of peacefulness came over Precious when she saw her daughter coming towards her. "Angel, It's wonderful to see you too," she smiled warmly, giving them both a hug.

"Mom, everything looks so beautiful."

"It really does," Angel nodded. "Our father would be pleased."

"I wanted to create something special for Nico," Precious exhaled, staring off at the unobstructed views of the ocean and bay. "He always talked about not finding a moment to just relax his mind. He never seemed to be able to escape his hectic and chaotic life in New York City. So, I thought Nico would love for us to celebrate his life here, at such a serene and beautiful place."

"I completely agree. You did such an amazing job putting this together, Precious. And that picture," Angel smiled adoringly at the photo of her, Aaliyah and their dad together, "Is my absolute favorite."

"It was Nico's favorite too," Precious beamed. "I remember the first time he told me about you.

Your father truly adored you, Angel. His eyes lit up whenever he spoke your name. He was so proud of you."

"Thank you for telling me that." Angel's eyes watered up.

"It's the truth. I just wish you all had more time together. He loved you so much."

"I loved him too. I still do. It doesn't seem real that he's gone."

"I know it must be overwhelming for you. First your husband and now your father. If you need anything," Precious placed Angel's hand in hers, "please let me know. We're all here for you. You're family...our family."

"Thank you. I wouldn't have been able to get through any of this without Aaliyah," Angel said, placing her head on her sister's shoulder.

"I told you, if we have each other, we can get through anything. We're the dynamic duo," Aaliyah stated proudly.

"Amen to that!" Angel exclaimed.

"Just the way Nico would want it," Precious grinned.

"Mom, we've spent all this time talking about how beautiful the décor is and you making sure we're okay, but what about you. How are you dealing with saying goodbye to your first love?"

Before Precious could answer, she became distracted, and her eyes were locked on the couple who just arrived. "Aaliyah, out of respect for your father please be polite," she said taking a deep breath.

Aaliyah and Angel both turned towards the entryway. Aaliyah's heart dropped. It was her first time seeing Amir and Justina since she rushed to the church to stop their wedding, but she was too late.

"Are you okay?" Angel questioned her sister, gently squeezing her hand.

"I will be." Aaliyah swallowed hard. "I assumed they would be here, but I guess I hadn't totally prepared myself. Seeing them up close and personal hits different," she admitted.

"Maybe you all should head inside for a moment, and have a glass of champagne," Precious suggested.

"That sounds like an excellent idea," Angel nodded. "Come on, Aaliyah." But before the sisters could make a quick exit, the newlyweds were in front of their face.

Amir made eye contact with each of the three women standing in front of him. "My heart is aching for you all over your loss," Amir stated benevolently. "Nico was a remarkable man. I learned quite a bit from him, and I'll always remember his words of wisdom. His presence will be missed but his spirit will live on."

"Thank you." Precious embraced Amir, moved by his kind words.

"Yes, thank you," Aaliyah and Angel chimed in.

"I'm so sorry for your loss too. I have many fond memories of Nico, especially as a little girl. He was always kind to me," Justina said sincerely.

"Thank you, Justina," Precious said, since Aaliyah and Angel remained silent.

"That's very kind of you to say, Justina. And congratulations on the nuptial. I wish you both the best." Aaliyah stated, surprising everyone with how gracious she was being to her archnemesis.

"We appreciate you saying that." Amir smiled.

"No problem. I would've come to the wedding, but I guess my invite got lost in the mail," she added, instantly turning the amiable mood tense. "I was joking," Aaliyah quickly said, noticing the sharp glare from her mother.

"Of course, you were. We knew that." Precious let out a slight laugh. "Where is that sweet baby?" she asked, wanting to immediately move past the touchy wedding topic.

"We thought it was best to let him stay home with the nanny. We've been traveling a lot and I could tell my lil' man needed the rest," Amir explained.

"I bet he is getting so big," Precious said excitedly. While she engaged in small talk with Amir, Angel used that opportunity to excuse herself to use the restroom, bringing Aaliyah with her.

"Good grief! I owe you for getting me away from those two. I was on the verge of vomiting if I had to stand there a second longer," Aaliyah complained.

"You hid your disdain very well." Angel nodded her head with approval.

"Except for that minor slipup."

"You recovered nicely and quickly. I believed you when you said you were joking," Angel winked, as she and Aaliyah both laughed all the way to the bathroom.

"Precious, you outdid yourself." Genesis stood on the terrace looking out at all the people who came to celebrate the life of Nico Carter. "Some of those pictures you have framed, I forgot we even took them," he gave a nostalgic laugh. "Brings back a lot of good memories."

"That was my intention. I wanted us to all be here together for Nico, but the one person I need the most right now isn't here," Precious sighed.

"I'm sure you're speaking of Supreme. Where is he?"

"I don't know," she admitted with resentment in her voice. "He called me about an hour ago, said he was running late because he had to take care of some business, but would be here shortly. I know Supreme and Nico weren't exactly close, but I believed he would show up to support me and Aaliyah."

"Supreme and Nico weren't close, and some would argue they didn't even like each other. But over the years they developed a mutual respect."

"Then why isn't Supreme here to show his respect?" she stared at Genesis searching for answers.

"Supreme was there when Nico got shot. Barely left his side while he was in the hospital."

"I know this, which is why I'm shocked he would choose this moment, such an important day to get ghost." Precious shook her head incensed.

"Guilt." Genesis stated.

"Guilt for what? Supreme didn't do anything wrong. Nico's death is on Maverick."

"You know that. I know that too, but Supreme is dealing with his own reality. I think in his mind, Supreme feels Nico died on his watch. Give him time. Supreme is dealing with his own form of grief," Genesis surmised.

"I never thought of that, but you've always been a wise man, Genesis." Precious got lost in her thoughts for a second, gazing out at the waves in the ocean. It brought her the inner peace she was desperately searching for. "Nico's death has been so unbelievably tragic. Here today, I wanted to give us a glimmer of hope that we would get through this."

Genesis placed his hand on her shoulder. "We will get through this. Nico wouldn't want it any other way."

"I know but when will it stop? I'm so fuckin' tired of the bloodshed. Losing Nico..." Precious put her head down and went silent for a moment. "It's too much."

"After we leave here, I'm putting Talisa and Genevieve on a plane," Genesis disclosed.

"What?" Precious was surprised by the admission. "Where are they going?"

"I still haven't decided. But someplace safe and far away from here. Because like you, I'm tired of the bloodshed too. I've survived in the game this long, but the clock runs out on all of us if we can't ever make a clean exit."

"Are you saying you're ready to get out the game?" Precious was curious to know.

"I don't think I'll ever be ready to leave the game. It's part of who I am but it's not about me anymore. I have to consider Talisa and my daughter. If I don't get out, there's a real chance I could end up dead or even worst they could."

"So, what's your next move?"

"Keep my family safe until Maverick is a dead man."

Chapter Three

We Belong Together

Mia had spent the morning watching Caleb sleep. It'd become her daily routine since she'd finessed her way into his bed. She still couldn't believe all her hard work and scheming had finally paid off. Murdering her sister wasn't part of Mia's original plan but when the opportunity presented itself, she knew it was the key to unlocking Caleb's heart. Now here she was, waking up to the love of her life. Mia hadn't left his side since she came knocking at Caleb's door with the news, that Celinda was dead, and it was all her doing.

She killed her only sibling to prove her love and loyalty to Caleb.

"Good morning handsome," Mia smiled.

"How is it you always wake up before me?" Caleb mumbled, stretching his arms.

"I told you, I'm an early bird." Mia continued to smile while sprinkling kisses down Caleb's chest, before putting her wet lips around his dick. She licked and sucked until he was rock hard. The intoxicating blowjob had also become a part of Mia's morning routine and Caleb welcomed it. Ejaculating shortly after waking up, seemed to take the edge off and put Caleb in a more optimistic mood. Plus, Mia seemed to enjoy tasting the discharge of his semen, which made the experience more pleasurable to him. Once done, she would lay her head on his chest as if they were a young married couple deeply in love. In her mind, they were. Caleb on the other hand was thinking it was time for Mia to beat it, because he had been on a break long enough. He needed to hit the street and get back to work, instead he was dozing off. But those thoughts were interrupted when Caleb heard a loud banging at the front door.

"Who tha fuck is that?" Caleb mumbled, reaching under his bed for his Glock 17. He made a gesture to Mia to stay there before he went to see who it was. The banging continued to get louder and louder. He looked out the window and let out a deep sigh before opening the door.

"Man, why you come to the door strapped?" Prevan scoffed.

"I was 'bout to fuck a nigga lungs up," Caleb taunted. "You know betta than bangin' on a man's door, especially first thing in the morning," he huffed.

"I been calling you for the last week and so has Ma. You ain't takin' no calls or responding to texts. I thought you might've been dead up in this bitch."

"Bro, ain't nobody dead," Caleb shrugged still posted in the doorway entrance. "I turned my phone off. I didn't wanna be disturbed."

"Are you gon' let me in or what?" Prevan questioned.

Caleb let out a heavy groan, moving out the way, so his brother could come inside. "So, what's the fuckin' emergency?" he asked already knowing what it was.

"It's Celinda." Prevan was shaking his head, face full of distress.

"You know I don't like that bitch. What about her?" Caleb sucked his teeth, expressing his disgust.

"She dead man. Celinda dead." Prevan was getting choked up. His eyes were watering. "You not gon' say nothin'?"

"What you want me to say...you want me to pretend like I care?"

"How you gon' be so cold?" Prevan sat down on the couch staring up at Caleb.

"Cold?! Are you serious? Celinda is the reason Floyd is dead."

"She didn't have nothin' to do wit' that. She swore on our daughter."

"Man, cause you a sucker for some pussy, don't put that on me like I'ma believe that dumb shit."

"Fuck you, Caleb! If you can't show no sympathy for Celinda, what about Amelia? Your niece loss her mother."

"Thank God she got her grandmother and you. Despite being sprung on a grimy hoe, you are a good father."

"We can't replace her mother, Caleb."

"So, you say. Is that it? Cause I got shit to do."

"Nah, I've been tryna reach Mia. Have you spoken to her? She needs to know about her sister."

"What about Celinda?" Mia came out of the

bedroom wearing one of Caleb's t-shirts. She tried to give the impression she hadn't been ear hustling the whole time.

Prevan looked over at Mia and then back at Caleb. "How long this been going on?"

"Bro, mind yo' business." Typically getting head in the morning made Caleb mellow, but even though she was dead, hearing Celinda's name fucked up his entire mood.

"Prevan, what about my sister?" Mia spoke up, wanting to prevent the brothers from continuing to exchange jabs, plus she was ready to get her fake grieving over with.

He grunted at Caleb and then focused his attention back on Mia. "There's no easy way to say this but Celinda..." Prevan's voice cracked.

"What about Celinda?" Mia walked closer.

"She's dead."

"Dead! Don't play with me like that!"

"Wish I was playin' Mia, but I ain't. Celinda is gone." A tear rolled down Prevan's face, which further infuriated Caleb.

"This nigga so bitch made," Caleb uttered under his breath. He watched with disdain as Prevan tried to console Mia, who was crying hysterically.

"How did this happen? Why is my sister

dead?" Mia asked between sobs.

"It's the craziest shit. They thinking it was some sort of allergic shock."

"You mean anaphylaxis?"

"What's that?" Prevan gave Mia a perplexed glare.

"It's a scientific term. I learned about it in one of my classes at school. It's a severe and sometimes life-threatening reaction that can develop within an hour or even seconds, after exposure to an allergen. It's like a substance to which an individual's immune system has become sensitized. Many allergens can touch off anaphylaxis like food, medications or even insect stings. So, what triggered Celinda's reaction?"

"I don't fuckin' know." Prevan placed his hands over his face. The doctors asked me if I knew what she might be allergic to, but I couldn't give them no answers. This shit is fuckin' crazy to me. I don't even know how to explain it to Amelia."

"I can't believe my sister's gone."

"I'm so sorry Mia, I know how tight you all were." Prevan held her close in his arms, while the stream of tears poured down Mia's face. "I'm putting together her funeral arrangements; any input would be appreciated."

"Of course. Anything you need. You can count

on me Prevan."

"Thank you. It'd be great if you stopped by to see Amelia. She's been asking for her Auntie Mia. We tried calling you but..."

"I recently changed my number," Mia stated cutting Prevan off. "Let me write down my new number for you. Tell Amelia I'll be by later today to see her."

"She'll love that," Prevan said, taking the piece of paper Mia handed him. "I'ma head out but Caleb hit me up when you done wit' not being disturbed. We do got business to handle."

"I'll give you time to mourn big brother," Caleb mocked as Prevan headed out.

"Mia, I'll see you later today," Prevan nodded, closing the door.

"Damn, if I didn't know better, I woulda thought those were real tears coming out yo' eyes," Caleb cracked, securing the double locks on the door. "Fuck that school shit, maybe you need to be an actress."

"I had to make it seem believable."

"You definitely did that. I almost forgot you were the one who murdered Celinda," Caleb sighed softly.

"But I did it for you and I would do it again." Mia had this wide-eyed deer in the headlight, paralyzed In surprise stare on her face.

While Mia stood in front of him with an aura of sweet innocence, Caleb's conscience remained at war. He didn't know if Mia was crazy in love with him, or simply a calculating disturbed young lady, who Caleb once believed was an angel in disguise.

Chapter Four

Shooter Interlude

Shiffon contemplated how the life altering events that caused her world to unravel seemed to have happened just last night. It was fresh in her mind. She had stood in the shadows waiting for Maverick to step out the SUV to board his chartered private jet. She had a gun pointed to his head, and with coolness and confidence, he gave her two options. Shiffon could either pull the trigger and watch Maverick die, or she could board the Cessna Citation X aircraft and disappear into the darkness with him.

The choice would seem clear, Shiffon was a well-paid assassin who had been hired to do a job...kill Maverick. The opportunity presented itself and all she needed to do was follow through on the course of action she'd committed to. But of course, there was one major problem, she had fallen deeply in love with her mark.

"It's easy to get lost in your thoughts out here," Maverick stated, glancing out at the South Pacific Ocean from the beachfront bures.

"It really is. Fiji Island is truly a tropical paradise. The tranquil environment makes it impossible to do anything else other than unwind."

The private resort was a romantic haven of natural beauty. Fringed by pristine white sandy beaches, captivating coral reefs, surrounded by crystal clear turquoise blue waters and cascading waterfalls. Amongst the secluded shores, towering palm trees silhouetted against the setting sun, lush gardens, breathtaking views and the seamless transition from indoor to outdoor living creating an entrancing serene yet luxurious atmosphere. On the flipside, there was also a gut-wrenching fear that Shiffon was unable to shake.

"Unwind is an interesting choice of words. You haven't been completely relaxed since we arrived. I figured after a few days of lounging by the plunge pool overlooking the lagoon, taking outdoor showers surrounded by tropical gardens, and the private fine dining on our deck would erase any stress you have. Or maybe the lack of intimacy between us, is what got you all tensed up," Maverick smiled.

"So, that's it...the lack of sex we're having, is what has me on edge?" Shiffon laughed.

"Hey, I don't know what else it could be," he casually shrugged. "I mean you said it yourself, this is a tropical paradise."

"True but taking a private plane and then a helicopter to a secluded island doesn't erase the fact that I was a hired shooter who didn't take the shot. Who knows what awaits me once I go back home."

"Who said I was letting you go back home?" Maverick took a few steps, narrowing the distance between them.

"I didn't realize this was a kidnapping," Shiffon gave him a quizzical gaze.

"It isn't. You chose to board the jet with me. It was your choice, so no I didn't kidnap you. But now that you're here, I'll decide when or if you leave."

"Are you joking? It's hard for me to tell when

it comes to you. You have a rather dark sense of humor."

"Did you know that a dark sense of humor is an indicator of high intelligence?"

"No, I didn't but if that's true, you must be a genius," Shiffon winked.

Maverick was now within reach of Shiffon, deleting all space between them. He gently placed his arm around her waist before aggressively pulling her close. Shiffon inhaled his masculine scent which was a mixture of expensive cologne and cognac. She wanted to melt in his arms but instead Shiffon swallowed hard trying to regain her composure.

"You seem a bit light on your feet, are you feeling okay?" he caressed the top of her sleeked back bun. But Shiffon remained silent, as if in a hypnotic trance. Maverick swept her up in his strong arms, carrying her across the glass bottom floor. He pushed open the hand-carved solid mahogany double doors leading into their personal sanctuary. He laid Shiffon down on the four-panel canopy bed with floor length delicately woven silk white drapes. Once you entered the master bedroom, the soaring ceilings throughout the villa was replaced with a retractable roof that slid back at the touch of a bottom, so you could lay in bed and stargaze. It was beyond mesmerizing and Maverick seemed to know it. He allowed Shiffon to savor the amorous moment before slowly slipping off the sleeveless metallic crochet cover up dress she was wearing. The material of the luxurious Egyptian cotton linen on the king-size bed felt sensuous and rich against her naked skin.

His touch was measured, more tactile and it made her entire body tingle as the sheet brushed against her erect nipples. There was hungry lust in his eyes, but he ignored the urge to engage in ravenous sex, he chose a more subtle lovemaking technique. He was considerate, taking his time and moving not too fast. Shiffon trailed her long fingers down his chiseled chest, longing to feel every inch of his dick inside of her. But he chose to let her see what his tongue could do first. Maverick had her pussy dripping wet and she wondered if it felt like a cascade of water was raining down on him. Her passionate cries of pleasure only heightened his determination to satisfy her every desire.

In the midst of bringing Shiffon to her first orgasm, Maverick put a cease to his tongue foreplay and glided his hardness deep inside her walls intensifying her climax. He brought his lips down on hers. One moment his kisses were tender the next, strong and assertive. He began exploring her mouth with his tongue. He was making her tremble with anticipation of what was to come next. She dug her nails into his skin, lost in his embrace. All rational thought deserted Shiffon when in Maverick's orbit. This was no ordinary love for her. If staying here with him at what she described as their personal tropical paradise would feed her appetite of being deeply in love, then Shiffon never wanted to go back home.

Chapter Five

Up At Night

Precious couldn't identify the exact moment it happened, but there had been an undeniable detachment between her and Supreme. Never one to shy away from conflict, she decided now was the perfect time to get answers.

"Glad you finally made it home. I was trying to stay up and I almost fell asleep," Precious said, sitting up in bed.

"You didn't have to wait up for me," Supreme replied, placing his wallet down on the nightstand by the bed.

"I had no choice. When I'm coming, you're going, and you stay gone. Are you purposedly keeping distance between us?"

"Precious, what are you talking about? It's too late and I'm too tired to engage in an unnecessary argument with you."

"Argument...I thought we were having a conversation, something we haven't done in weeks," Precious stated sharply. "You never even explained to me why you didn't show up to Nico's homegoing ceremony."

"I told you I got caught up in handling some business."

"The same business that's keeping you from coming home at night?" she responded with a sudden flash of anger, flinging the duvet covering her legs.

"Precious, calm down. I've been putting in a lot of hours with this new project I'm working on, but I always come home."

"Yeah, to sleep and by the time I wake up you're right back out the door. What type of fuckin' new project is this?" she asked in an accusatory tone. "It seems to be life changing."

"It has the potential to be," Supreme said evenly. Precious wasn't sure if he was being serious or simply mocking her, so she went on the defense.

"Are you having an affair? And don't bullshit me!"

"No," he said quietly. "I'm tired. I just wanna take a shower and go to bed," Supreme responded calmly, and headed to the bathroom.

Precious stayed silent. Their conversation did not accomplish what she hoped. Instead of her suspicion and anger dissolving, it had evolved. After so many years of being married and just in each other's lives, they shared a connection and Precious could normally figure out what was going on with Supreme, but this time she was stuck. They had been through the storm too many times to count, but always found their way back to each other. So, Precious didn't want to believe her husband was having an affair. But there was one irrefutable rule life had taught her, always follow your gut instincts. When you don't make the most of your own innate wisdom, you can end up with tragic results.

"Any word on Maverick?" Genesis questioned Roland, one of his most trusted lieutenants within his drug operation.

T-Roc had taken a seat at the table, anxious to hear what Roland had to say. He was there to strategize with Genesis as to what their next move should be. Knowing their enemy's whereabouts would prove helpful with how they should maneuver.

"That nigga like a ghost," Roland grunted. "His chartered Gulfstream jet left Atlanta and landed in Los Angeles. After that, I don't know where he went," he explained. "I even have some people that do security at LAX, and they can't find no further data on that flight."

"How is that possible?" Genesis inquired.

"More than likely they landed at a private airport on an unlisted flight," Roland revealed.

"That sounds like some slick shit Maverick would do," T-Roc shook his head. "Always one step ahead."

"We need to figure out how to cut that nigga off at the knees," Genesis said flatly. "Because he might be laying low right now, but he will be back to finish the damage he started."

"What about his two righthand men, Micah and Cam...any word on their whereabouts?" T-Roc asked impatiently. "If we track them down, they might lead us to their boss."

"They MIA too," Roland said with an exasperated sigh.

"If only that fuckin' assassin had done what she was hired to do," Genesis seethed, his expression hardening.

"What happened with that anyway?" T-Roc had been waiting for an update.

"Last time I spoke with Caleb, he said he was trying to get the woman on the phone. I haven't heard anything, so my guess is, he hasn't had much luck," Genesis presumed. "I'll reach back out to him to see what's going on. But we need answers. I find it troubling that this man continues to elude us."

"I do too, but boss I'm on it," Roland assured Genesis, standing up from the table. "I need to head over to the warehouse in the Bronx, but I will track down Maverick. We'll get him," he nodded confidently on his way out the door.

"I wish I felt as self-assured as Roland," T-Roc scoffed, stretching out his long legs under the conference table. "There's no tellin' where that muthafucka might be. And speakin' of muthafuckas, where the hell is Supreme? He hasn't returned any of my calls. I thought for sure he would show up for this meeting today."

"So did I." Genesis let out a heavy sigh. "Not sure what's going on with Supreme. He's been off since Nico got shot. I think he's taking Nico's death hard."

"I get it but this ain't the time to go off the grid. We need all the manpower we can gather up, or Nico won't be the last person we bury within our inner circle." T-Roc's words resonated with Genesis.

"I can't let that happen." Genesis stood in front of the floor to ceiling window, staring out at the New York City skyline, not even cognizant that his fists were balled. Anger consumed him and he was ready to fight but his opponent remained out of his reach.

"Man, it already happened. We buried Nico," T-Roc scoffed as if Genesis needed a reminder. "We can't find that nigga Maverick. I don't wanna accept this bullshit either, but facts are facts and our options have run out."

"Fuck that." Genesis turned around giving T-Roc a long hard look. "I haven't utilized all my options."

"Really?" he said raising an eyebrow. "What option is this because so far we runnin' in circles," T-Roc said swiveling in his chair interested in what Genesis would say next.

"Silvano Cattaneo." Genesis exhaled sharply.

"Silvano...you haven't mentioned him in

years. After what went down, I thought I'd never hear his name come out your mouth again."

"That was the plan, but extreme circumstances can compel change. This is one of those situations," Genesis reasoned.

"I hear you but..."

"But nothing," Genesis interrupted T-Roc, knowing a warning would follow. "Silvano has a long reach, much longer than mine. He'll be able to locate Maverick."

"True...but."

"I don't wanna hear your buts," Genesis fumed, cutting T-Roc off again. "You said it yourself, we've run out of options. That nigga done had me up at night one too many times. I ain't burying nobody else I love. The next funeral I'm attending, is when Maverick dies."

Chapter Six

Path To Revenge

Angel was sitting outside on the balcony of Aaliyah's upper east side high rise apartment. There was a cool summer breeze that made her think of being back in Miami. Sadness soon followed but all Angel could do was embrace her memories and then let go.

"I should've known this is where I'd find you," Aaliyah said cheerfully, joining her sister outside.

"You know how much I adore the layout of your apartment, but this spot right here is my absolute favorite. You can't beat this view," Angel remarked.

"No, you can't! This view was one of the major selling points for me too," Aaliyah admitted, taking a seat next to her sister on the off-white chaise lounge. "I know how much you love them, so I made you one too," she smiled, handing Angel one of her freshly made smoothies.

"I needed this," Angel said with anticipation of taking her first sip. "I always know I'm getting my daily recommended dose of fruits and vegetables when I drink one of these."

"I agree. I feel a lot less guilty about devouring my favorite desserts and washing them down with one of my Starbuck lattes," she cracked with a slight giggle. "So, I was thinking," Aaliyah said ready to jump to the next topic. "They're having the grand opening of this new boutique on Lexington Avenue. We should go be nosey, plus I need some new shoes."

"I've seen your massive closet, you don't need anything, especially not new shoes," Angel laughed.

"I suppose *need* is the wrong word," she shrugged. "But I still wanna go."

"I'm sure you do," Angel glanced over at her sister grinning widely. "Actually, I could use some shop therapy right now, but I have to meet with someone in an hour, so you'll have to spend your money without me."

"Meet someone...I didn't think you knew anyone in NYC. Who are you meeting?" Aaliyah had no shame when it came to prying for information.

"It's in regard to some business I'm considering doing."

"What business? I have a lot of time on my hand, is it a business opportunity we can do together? Like be partners," Aaliyah suggested with excitement.

"It's not that sort of business." It was obvious Angel was holding back but that didn't deter Aaliyah from pushing harder for more details. "Honestly, I would rather not get you involved. The less you know the better."

Aaliyah placed her smoothie down on the natural stone tabletop and leaned closer to Angel. "Girl, we're sisters. Whatever you're involved in, I need to be involved in it too. I'm serious...don't hold back."

Angel let out a heavy sigh. She was reluctant to confide in Aaliyah, mainly because she didn't want her sister trying to change her mind. But she also knew she could trust her and whatever they discussed would remain between the two of them.

"I tracked down someone who can lead me to the man responsible for Darien's murder. I'll finally be able to get justice for my husband."

"I had no idea you were even working on that. I thought you were letting the police handle it. Why didn't you tell me?" Aaliyah asked.

"Because I didn't want you to try and stop me. I figured it was best to let you and everyone else believe I was going to allow the police to do their job. Which I am, but I'm also doing mine."

"Why would I stop you from seeking retribution for your husband? I would've done the same thing for Dale, but Arnez, the monster responsible for his murder, is already dead. So, I completely understand your desire to make whoever did this pay."

"Thank you. Your support means a lot and so does your understanding." Angel wrapped her arms around Aaliyah. "I won't be able to have a peaceful night sleep until I bring down everyone who has my husband's blood on their hands."

"I don't want to support you from a distance. I want to be right by your side. Let me come with you to meet this person."

Angel was debating whether this was a good

idea or not. She was hesitant to accept Aaliyah's offer. "Maybe you should sit this one out."

"Listen, I'm just as protective of you as you are of me. That's why we need to do this together. I have your back and you have mine. This is an extremely emotional time for you. You need that added buffer, which is me. Let me do this with you," Aaliyah implored.

"Just know if you take this journey with me, once we start, there's no turning back. Are you prepared for that? Because the path to revenge can get extremely ugly." Angel wanted to be completely transparent about the potential danger they faced.

"I won't be turning back. I'm all in." Aaliyah did a pinky promise with Angel and the two sisters vowed to take the path of revenge together.

"Thanks for coming over baby," Caleb's mother said, putting down some fresh out the dryer towels she was folding. "It's always good to see you." She kissed her son on the cheek.

"It's good to see you too Ma. What's goin' on?"

"I can't believe how fast you got over here.

Can I make you a plate? Prevan and Amelia left not too long ago. I made them some dinner," she said, walking towards the kitchen.

"Nah, I'm good," Caleb spoke up to stop his mom from leaving out the living room.

"Are you sure?"

"Positive. Mia and I about to go have dinner."

"Oh really...you going to pick her up after you leave here?"

"Nah, she waitin' for me in the car."

"Why didn't you bring her in? You know how much I like Mia," she smiled warmly.

"Ma, when you called me, you made it sound like it was an emergency I get over here. I didn't think it was no need for Mia to come in. So, what's up?" Caleb's voice now had a hint of impatience.

"Sit down, baby." Caleb's mother sat down on the couch across from her son. "I'm worried about you and your brother."

"Is that what you called me over here for?" Caleb sucked his teeth, rising from the recliner chair. "I'm rushin' to get over here, thinkin' something wrong and you straight," he exhaled deeply.

"Something *is* wrong. It breaks my heart to see my sons at odds. Enough of this!" She shouted. "Now sit back down."

Caleb grudgingly did what his mother asked.

He was ready to go and the longer he felt forced to stay, the more resentful he was becoming. "I don't have a problem wit' Prevan, I just don't want to deal wit' him," Caleb shrugged.

"How you not gonna deal with your own brother? He's the only sibling you have."

"I also had another brother. His name was Floyd. You remember him. He would bring you money, groceries and shit whenever you needed something," Caleb spit. "Floyd was murdered because of that trifling bitch Celinda."

"I get you upset about Floyd; I miss him too. But you can't cut off your brother because he chose to believe the mother of his child. Celinda said she had nothing to do with Floyd's death. Besides none of that matters now, Celinda is dead too and your brother is hurting. So is your niece."

"I'll always be there for my niece and Prevan too but that don't mean I need to deal wit' him like that. He always chose that no good..." Caleb stopped himself from going all the way in on Celinda. "The point is, when Celinda was alive, Prevan's loyalty was to her, not me. So, don't ask me to welcome him with open arms now that she's dead and he feels alone."

"Can you at least try to mend the relationship with your brother?" she asked, waiting patiently for Caleb to answer her question but he kept his head down, not saying a word. "I'm asking as your mother. Please do it for me," she pleaded.

A twinge of penitence shot through Caleb. When he lifted his head up, his mother had dejection in her eyes and that cut Caleb to the core. She always tried to appear strong and unbreakable, so to see her on the verge of tears hit different.

"Okay."

"Okay what?" her eyes widened with cautious optimism.

"I'll work on mending my relationship wit' Prevan."

"Thank you, baby." She went over and hugged Caleb with all her might.

"But Ma, let me do this on my time...okay."

"Okay, I can do that," she nodded.

"Thank you." Caleb stared down at his mother because she only came to his chest. "I gotta go," he said, wiping away the tear that escaped her eye. He bent down and placed a kiss on her forehead before walking out the door.

Caleb stood on the front porch for a moment and inhaled a sweet pungent zing as the winds picked up and the clouds rolled. It was a familiar sharp, fresh aroma that came before the rain begins. He glanced up at the large portion of sunlight, coloring the sky in different shades of orange and red. There was a soft glow as the last shimmer of daylight left the sky and dusk had begun to set in. When he took his first step down the stairs is when he noticed the dark SUV parked across the street. Caleb reached in the back of his jeans to retrieve his Kimber Rapide semi-auto pistol. Although he would prefer not to have a shootout on the block his mother lived on, he wasn't ready to die on her front porch either. When the back door opened to the SUV, with his finger placed firmly on the trigger, he raised his weapon ready to fire.

"Damn, you hard to track down," Amir shouted, walking across the street towards Caleb.

Caleb sighed softly, relieved shots weren't about to be ringing through the air. "Bruh, you had me out here 'bout to be trigger happy. You can't be pullin' up on a nigga like that," he chuckled, bending at the waist, as they leaned into each other for a one-armed hug.

"What's good, Caleb? You can go 'head and put that gun away. I come in peace," Amir greeted Caleb with a jovial tone.

"I'm here, so I'm straight."

"No doubt."

"What brings you to Philly? Don't tell me the honeymoon already over?" Caleb joked.

"The Mrs. is actually in Miami. I stopped through to see you before I head there myself," Amir explained. "You hard to track down. My father told me I couldn't step foot in Florida until we made contact. So here I am."

"Man, I know Genesis pissed wit' me." Caleb shook his head. "Since Floyd's murder, I just been goin' through some shit. I know business don't stop, but my mind was all over the place and I didn't want to fuck shit up."

"I understand. Trust me I been there. How are you feeling now...are you ready to get back to work?"

"Fo' sure. The streets been callin' my name and I'm ready to answer."

"Pleased to hear," Amir nodded. "We need you. Philly is one of our largest territories and you're an excellent earner. It's short notice but can you handle us having a large shipment come in on Friday?"

"Of course. I got you covered."

"Good, I'll let my father know. He also wanted me to ask you about something else...make that someone," Amir clarified.

"Who?"

"The assassin you hired."

"Shiffon, yeah I haven't been able to get in touch with her," Caleb revealed.

"When was the last time you all spoke?"

"The day she was supposed to murder Maverick at the airport in Atlanta."

"That didn't happen. Do you think he got to her instead?"

"Like she dead...fuck I ain't even consider that." Caleb wondered if there was reason to worry. Maybe something bad did happen to Shiffon.

"Is it typical for her to be out of touch?" Amir asked.

Caleb thought about the question for a second. "Not when she's under contract for a job."

"So, this is out of character for her?"

"Yeah, it is."

"Well, let me know if you hear from her."

"What about Maverick? Any news on him 'cause that nigga problematic."

"Yep, he is but my father is working on something. Maverick will get got. It's only a matter of time. But until then, watch yo' back," Amir said glancing down at his watch. "I need to get going. I believe I have enough time to make my flight. I'll be in touch but if you find out anything before then, hit me up."

"Will do." Caleb headed towards his car watching Amir get back inside the SUV and drive off. "Mia, sorry I had you waitin' in here all this time," he said closing the car door.

"It's okay, I know you have a lot going on. Are we still going out for dinner?"

"Yeah, I'm starvin'. I just need to make a call first. Damn, it's still going straight to voicemail." Caleb's face frowned up.

"What's wrong...who are you trying to get in touch with?"

"Shiffon," he said, calling her back again. "Fuck, I hope she's alright.

Mia listened intently while Caleb left a voice message for Shiffon. He then continued to call her relentlessly, almost as if he couldn't stop himself. His behavior made it obvious to Mia that he cared for this woman. *I wonder if Shiffon is the woman who attended Caleb's birthday party and he couldn't keep his eyes or hands off her,* Mia thought to herself. She considered asking Caleb but didn't want to venture into interrogation territory. She knew coming across as a whiny, jealous lover would not score her any points with him. But she decided it was best for Shiffon to stay missing, because if she returned, Mia would have no choice but to eliminate the competition.

Chapter Seven

Making Inroads

Shiffon had been procrastinating checking her voicemail and text messages. Being in Fiji with Maverick was the escape she needed but living in a fantasy world had a short shelf life. It was time to face reality.

"Caleb hi. Did I catch you at a bad time?"

"Yo, you have no idea how happy I am to hear your fuckin' voice. Where you been…I was startin' to think you was dead or some foul shit like that," Caleb griped.

"I'm sorry. I didn't mean to worry you," Shiffon said, looking over her shoulder making sure Maverick was still inside the bungalow while she was outside on the covered deck speaking to Caleb.

"Where are you and why has your phone been turned off?"

"There was a family emergency with my mother and little brother. It required my full attention, and I couldn't have any distractions." Shiffon had practiced her lie long before placing this phone call to Caleb.

"Is your mother and brother okay...they not hurt, are they?"

"No!" Shiffon blurted out. There was so much concern in Caleb's voice that it made her consumed with guilt over the blatant lie she told him. "Everyone's good, including me."

"Man, after all this time of not hearing from you, I was beginning to think Maverick took you out. But he still alive and you still alive, so what went down that night?"

"Nothing. A terrible accident involving my mother and brother happened, so I couldn't make it to the airport in time."

"So, you never saw Maverick that night?"

"No. I never saw him. I know I let you down and I'm sorry, but I had to be there for my family."

"You ain't neva gotta apologize for puttin' yo' family first. You still in Atlanta, are you back to work...what's goin' on wit' you?"

"I'm home but my family still needs me. I should be back to work in a couple weeks."

"Take yo' time. I can relax now that I know you safe."

"What about Maverick?" she asked.

"What about him?"

"When I get back to work does Genesis want me to finish the job he hired me to do?" Shiffon was probing for information but had to be careful not to risk raising suspicion. She was in love with Maverick and wanted to protect him at all costs.

"I'm not sure. Genesis is workin' on something, but I don't have no details, at least not yet."

"Got it." Shiffon stated flatly. "I'll be in touch when I'm back to work. Take care, Caleb." She ended the call and let out a heavy sigh. Shiffon struggled with how she'd be able to pull this off. Juggling this persona of being a team player for Caleb and maintaining her intimate relationship with Maverick. It seemed impossible, but she was determined to figure out a way to make it work, because Shiffon refused to let go of the man she had falling in love with.

Genesis' driver pulled the infinite black Lucid Air Dream Edition into a "No Standing Zone," directly in front of Caliente restaurant. It was a hotspot where mobsters would do business—or simply hold court for their loyal subjects. It was equivalent to what the legendary Sparks Steakhouse was in the 1980's. Genesis was there to meet with Silvano the head of the Cattaneo crime family. His driver remained in the car, while Rolando accompanied Genesis inside the restaurant.

Many considered Silvano to be the capo di tutti capi—boss of all bosses. For Genesis, he was a means to an end. When they arrived, Silvano was flanked with two Sicilian bodyguards sitting with him in a patio area.

"It is wonderful to see you, my friend." Silvano stood up, with his signature cigar stuck in his mouth, wrapping his arms around Genesis. "Please sit down and have some chianti." Although he wasn't interested in sharing wine with Silvano, Genesis allowed him to pour a glass out of respect.

"Thank you." Genesis took a small sip of the wine before putting the glass down and pushing it to the side.

"You can only imagine my pleasant surprise when I received your call. It had been way too long, my friend."

"Can you blame me, Silvano. I always considered you to be a man of your word, but you proved me wrong."

"I don't remember it exactly that way." Silvano took a puff from his cigar.

"Not sure why. Your men caused a major shipment to be intercepted by the U.S. Coast Guard. Two of my men took full responsibility. Never snitched. To show your gratitude you promised to reimburse the money I lost from that deal and give me a price break on the next shipment."

"Yes, I recall that," Silvano acknowledged, taking a bite of his succulent steak.

"In the following weeks, I was arrested on some separate charges but was released shortly after. During my brief stint in jail, not only did you give my product away, but you also sold it to my biggest competitor. And you never returned my money. That same competitor believed I was now in a position of weakness and used it as an opportunity to take over all my territories in New York. I had to go to war behind what you did, Silvano."

"A war you won."

"No thanks to you," Genesis shot back.

Silvano inhaled and exhaled deeply. For the first time during their lunch, he took the cigar out of his mouth and placed it to rest on the ashtray. "My friend," he paused before continuing. "It was never my intention to cross you."

Genesis wanted to crack his skull every time Silvano referred to him as "my friend." But he remained focused on getting what he needed from someone he once considered a trusted business associate.

"But you did cross me, which is why I stand by what I said, you're not a man of your word."

"I did not cross you but," Silvano held up his index finger. "I did not honor our agreement and for that I owe you an apology. Unfortunately, my son Gabriel made a side deal without my knowledge or consent. He would've ended up dead if I had stepped in and honored our agreement. You're a father. Surely you can understand loyalty to my son," he rationalized.

"I do understand but it's irrelevant at this juncture. The only reason I contacted you is because I need something, and I believe you can deliver. Besides, you owe me, which means you're inclined to do what I ask."

"Tell me what you need." Silvano folded his hands, placing them on the table listening to Genesis attentively.

"Maverick McClay. He does go by other aliases and uses different last names, but I was able to confirm this is the name on his official birth certificate. A few weeks ago, he chartered a jet from Atlanta to LA. I don't know where he went after that. I need you to find this man and kill him. The sooner the better, as he has caused a consequential amount of devastation on the people I love. He must be stopped before he can do anymore."

"Genesis, I always respected how you conduct yourself. If I'm able, I will do what you ask but it's not because I owe you, although I do. But I have my own motives. We did exceptional business together. It's my hope it can resume once I've honored your request. Will you at least consider it?"

"Yes, I will consider it," Genesis agreed. Silvano extended his arm, and the two men shook on it.

Chapter Eight

Unmasking The Façade

Precious sat in the midtown office of the private investigator she hired to find out what the hell was going on with her husband. Heartache and rage consumed her entire body as she scrolled through the pictures the P.I. had taken. She didn't want to believe it, but she was holding the proof in her hands.

"Single family home, minivan, all the trappings of a readymade family. Do they share a child together?" Precious practically choked asking the question but she wanted to know.

"I don't believe so," the P.I. shook his head. "I haven't seen a child, but I've only been watching the house for a couple days. Your husband is a hard man to track. He did an excellent job keeping this woman and her location under wraps. It was by pure accident and a little bit of luck that I found both. I can keep doing some digging and continue to watch the house if you like."

"No, I can take it from here. I have the evidence I need to confront my husband." Precious grabbed the photos and stormed out the office. "You sonofabitch!" She wailed once in the privacy of her vehicle. Precious wanted to breakdown in tears over Supreme's betrayal but remained resilient. But instead of confronting Supreme, she decided to go directly to the other woman. Precious wouldn't leave that house until she found out how long this mystery chick had been fuckin' her husband.

Angel and Aaliyah's flight slowly began its descent into Miami International Airport. There was a perfect aerial view of Downtown Miami and the Florida Coastline. As the aircraft approached, they were greeted with lucent skies and glorious palm trees.

"South Beach here we come," Aaliyah said, followed with a wicked giggle.

"I wasn't expecting to return home so soon, but it's for a notable cause," Angel smiled.

"I like how you used that term notable to describe the adventure we're embarking on."

"This isn't what I would describe as an adventure, mainly given the danger that comes with it. It also concerns me that you haven't shown any signs of being terrified." Angel glanced over at Aaliyah who appeared to be oblivious to her uneasiness.

"You worry too much."

"I don't think you worry enough," Angel countered. "Aaliyah, we're putting you out there as bait to a mobster. And not just any mobster. The son of the head of the Cattaneo crime family. So, being scared would seem normal under the circumstances."

"In fairness, you were willing to be the bait, but Gabriel Cattaneo has seen you before and he's aware you were married to Darien. Since we know he has a proclivity for beautiful black women, I agreed to step in and get shit done," Aaliyah winked.

Angel sat back in her seat while the airplane

taxied around the corners on the airport tarmac upon landing. She admired how fearless Aaliyah seemed to be, but she was also nervous. When they met with the informant who was able to give them the name of the man responsible for her husband's death, the light that had dimmed inside Angel was once again lit. A surge of confidence that retribution was finally within her grasp made her even more calculating on how they would execute their plan. Because more than likely, this would be their one and only chance to kill Gabriel Cattaneo.

"Open the fuck up!" Precious hollered, pounding her fists against the double hardwood door with white trim and white pillars. She tried to peep through the triple glazed textured glass but couldn't see shit which infuriated her even more. "I got something for this bitch," she fumed, breathing fire. Precious walked back to her car to retrieve her Glock. If the woman wouldn't voluntarily open the door, then she would shoot her way in. Precious headed back up the classic front door staircase made of natural stone, purposedly kicking over the red flowers in terra-cotta pots.

"This the last warning!" Precious yelled thumping her foot against the door so hard it sounded like an explosion erupted. "Open this fuckin' door or I'ma shoot it open!"

The woman didn't want the smoke, because the second she heard that click clack sound from the gun, the door slightly opened. "Put that gun away or I'll call the police."

Precious was breathing heavy. She wanted to kick her way in, so she could see the woman lurking behind the door. "Are you willing to take the chance that I won't kill you before the police get here?"

The woman attempted to close the door back shut but Precious was not going to let that happen. She pressed forward using all her body weight, forcing her way in. Her push was so powerful, the woman fell back hitting the entryway floor.

"What do you want...why are you doing this?!" the woman was distraught, and she had reason to be. There was a crazed lady holding a gun standing over her.

"I'm not gonna shoot you," Precious finally said in an attempt to put the woman at ease, so she would cooperate and run her mouth. When she was putting the Glock in her purse, she noticed there were several missed calls from Supreme. *I bet this bitch was calling Supreme to save her ass while I was trying to break the door down,* Precious thought to herself. "Listen," she groaned. "I just need you to answer some questions for me."

"What questions do you have?"

"You can get up from the floor. I told you, I'm not gonna shoot you and I'm not gon' put my hands on you either," Precious sighed. "I give you, my word."

The woman got up from the floor, even though she was not convinced that the lady standing in front of her would keep her word. "Can you please tell me what questions you have so you can leave."

"How long have you been having an affair with my husband?"

"An affair with your husband..." A grimaced expression spread across the woman's face.

"Yeah bitch, an affair. You know when a woman is in a relationship with a married man. Clearly more than just fuckin' is going on since he got you living up in this house," Precious scolded, glancing around the 3-level house that came equipped with a servicing elevator. There were walls of windows and glass doors that gave a view of the lake that was only a few steps away. Precious began to have visions of Supreme and the woman having romantic candlelight dinners outside on the private deck overlooking the water, and she wanted to vomit.

"I am not having an affair with your husband or anybody else's husband," the woman stated with indignation. "Now can you please leave."

"I'm not going anywhere until you tell me the fuckin' truth, what is going on with you and my husband!" Precious shouted. "And since we're married, this house also belongs to me," she spewed. "Let me give myself a tour so I can see how *my* husband has been spending *our* money!"

"Please don't do this!" The woman cried out as Precious took off, headed in the direction of the master ensuite. But she knew it was a waste of her time, because there was no stopping the merciless lady.

"So, this is where you've been spending all your time when you're not home with me...your wife," Precious mumbled, fighting back tears while stomping through the house. When she came upon the master ensuite on the main level, she hesitated to go inside knowing she would see the bed Supreme was having sex in with another woman. But she was determined to confront her pain. Precious put her hand on the doorknob and slowly turned it. When she entered the room there was a familiar scent. Then she noticed something she wasn't expecting, a wheelchair.

Precious forged ahead passing the wheelchair on her way towards the open glass sliders leading to the balcony. The breeze from the lake sent a chill down her spine or was there another explanation for the shivering that was exhausting her spirit. Once she stepped outside, her body completely shut down. Precious fell to her knees and passed out.

Chapter Nine

Survival

"I love you," Shiffon turned to Maverick and uttered sweetly. It was the first time she had ever said those words to him out loud. She had voiced them plenty of times to herself, but she needed Maverick to know, although Shiffon knew in her heart he already did.

"I love you also. And before you ask, no I'm not saying it because you said it first. "I love you Shiffon, and I want you to be with me, but that might be asking too much of you," Maverick conceded.

Shiffon curled up her naked body next to Maverick before placing her head on his bare chest. Her expressive eyes flashing signals of deep lust and eternal love. "I want to be with you too...always."

"Are you willing to give up the life you've made for yourself?"

"You mean my life as a respected assassin," she teased, batting her long eyelashes.

"Hey, you might enjoy trackin' people down and killin' 'em. I'm not in a position to judge given my profession. My point is, you've made a life for yourself. Being with me would change all that."

"I know but I believe the love we share makes it worth it. This is the life I want—a life with you."

"Baby, I want the same." Maverick tilted his head down unable to resist her tempting lips. He kissed Shiffon and kissed her again. They were about to make love, but an indistinct noise interrupted them.

"Did you hear that?" Shiffon lifted her head.

"It's probably Micah. I thought he was sleep but maybe he got up."

"That's right, I forgot he was staying here for the next couple days. I also keep forgetting he's in the room directly next to us," she smiled getting back to kissing Maverick. But now his ears were on alert and that faint noise had become impossible to ignore.

"Stay here," Maverick spoke softly putting his finger over his mouth. He stepped out of bed and went to the door, pressing his ear against it. He immediately went to the closet and retrieved his guns, tossing one to Shiffon. As if in tandem, the gun Maverick tossed to Shiffon, landed on the bed at the decisive moment a thunderous boom palpitated through the bungalow. And once the gunfire erupted, unspeakable carnage would be the aftermath.

Precious opened her eyes in a daze. Her vision was a tad blurry, but she could see there was a ceiling fan above her. "What...what happened?" she stuttered, struggling to get her thoughts in focus. Precious glanced around the room and realized she was laying on top of a bed. Suddenly flashes of recent events flooded her mind and the truth began to emerge. She was only knocked out for a few minutes but when she first woke up, it felt like a lifetime.

"You're awake," the familiar face said, standing near the bed.

"Where is he?"

"Where is who?"

"Woman, don't play games with me." Precious mental and physical strength were basically back at one hundred, so she was unwilling to entertain the bullshit.

"If this is about your husband, I already told, I'm not having an affair with him."

"You know what tha fuck I'm talkin' about!" Precious shouted. She was about to knock the woman out, but then he appeared.

"Kyra, I can take it from here," he said, coming into the bedroom in the wheelchair Precious remember seeing before she passed out.

Precious buried her face in the palm of her hands, taking a second to process what was presently unfolding in front of her. She then ran to him. Kneeling on the floor, placing her head in his lap and draping her arms around his body.

"Nico, my forever love is alive," she wept before bursting into tears powerless to control her anguish but also elation that Nico was very much alive. He gently rubbed her back, wanting to placate the shock she understandably was in.

"Precious look at me," he said lifting her chin, staring into her bloodshot eyes and dilated pupils. Her face was strained, red and puffy. "I never wanted you to find out this way. I'm sorry," Nico said sincerely.

"But why...why did you make us believe you were dead?" she asked between sobs.

"Look at me...I'm bound to a wheelchair but by the Grace of God, I am alive. I still can't walk but it was much worst initially. I didn't think I was going to survive my injuries, neither did the doctor. But there was a procedure I could have. It was still experimental, with no proven track record. The risk was astronomical with little to no guarantee I would even survive the surgery. I didn't care about the probability, I wanted to move forward with the procedure, but I couldn't continue to put you all through an emotional rollercoaster."

"We would've wanted to be there for you. We're your family...we love you."

"I know but I didn't want that for any of you. This was my fight to win or lose."

"Once you survived the surgery, why didn't you tell us the truth then? Instead of continuing to allow us to think you were dead, having us mourn you?"

"After the surgery the doctor had to put me in a medically induced coma. They needed to protect my brain from swelling. I was in the ICU on a ventilator while they monitored the EEG until my brain activity was on point. I was so fuckin' weak. If it wasn't for Supreme and Kyra, I wouldn't have survived."

"Supreme? What does he have to do with this?" Precious was baffled.

"Who do you think put all this together for me. The surgery, getting this house, hiring Kyra and the other staff that has been helping with my rehabilitation. That was all Supreme."

"All this time Supreme knew you were alive and never said a word?" Precious felt blindsided.

"He did and that shit been eatin' him up. I knew he hated lying to everybody, but I insisted, this was the way it had to be." Nico stated sternly. "Supreme agreed to give me three more months. After that, if he felt he had to tell it, then so be it."

"Nico, I don't understand what you were waiting for!" Precious was shaking her head disdainfully. "You were alive...what was three more months going to do?"

"For one, give me time to learn how to fuckin' walk again! Do you think this is how I wanted to make my comeback...in a fuckin' wheelchair? I wanted to stand up and embrace my daughters, not have them bend down to hug me!" He scoffed.

"I don't care about that, and I know for a fact

Aaliyah and Angel won't."

"But I care!" He barked. "I fuckin' care." Nico exhaled deeply. "I'm grateful to be alive but I also want my *life* back."

"Your life is with your family. Not here, living in some house away from the people who love you. Supreme might've kept your secret but I won't. I'm telling Aaliyah you're alive."

"No, you won't." Supreme declared standing in the doorway eyeing Precious and Nico.

"How long have you been there listening?" Precious asked sharply.

"Long enough to know that telling Aaliyah or anyone else is off the table." He remained steadfast in his position.

Precious rose and walked towards Supreme with purpose in her stride. Her emotions were raw. She showed up ready to confront the woman she believed was having an affair with her husband, only to find out Nico was very much alive. Now that she knew the truth, she was determined to bring an end to this masquerade and Nico nor Supreme would be able to stop her.

Chapter Ten

Mrs. Blackwell

"There's my lil' man!" Desmond reached for his son who was smiling excitedly and clapping his hands.

When Desi babbled, "Miss da-da," Desmond's heart melted.

"I told you he missed you," Justina smiled warmly, handing him a happy yet fussy Desi. "By the way, he is also very sleepy." She wanted to give Desmond a heads up.

"I missed him too. More than I even thought possible," he said, looking forward to spending some quality time with Desi for the next week. "I'll put him down for a nap shortly. I just want to hold my lil' man for a minute. And thanks again for bringing him a couple days early. I appreciate the additional time," Desmond added.

"Of course. Our trip to New York fell during your visitation week and you agreed to let us take Desi. I guess the extra days is my way of saying thank you," Justina said sweetly.

"Did you want to come in for a few minutes while I put Desi down for a nap?"

"Sure, my hair appointment isn't for another hour. You might need my help putting him to sleep," Justina giggled as she followed Desmond to Desi's bedroom.

"Really?" he gave Justina a playful grin. "I thought I was the one who had the magic touch when it comes to getting Desi to take his nap."

"Whatever, that's not how I remember it," she teasingly shoved Desmond's arm. For a moment it felt like they were still married, living happily ever after as a family. Justina was having to stop herself more and more because her ex-husband had that effect on her.

To Justina it still felt as if they had only finalized their divorce recently, but in reality, it'd been almost a year. Initially, because she was so full of rage over her husband not only cheating on her with Dominique but creating a baby in the process, she refused to be around him. She let the lawyers hammer out the divorce settlement and allowed their shared nanny to facilitate the visitation agreement. But one weekend when Amir was out of town for business and the nanny was home sick, Justina had to drop Desi off herself. The moment she was alone with Desmond, all the fury she had been harboring diminished. Keeping her distance had helped to suppress her feelings, but Justina was still very much in love with her ex-husband although she was now married to Amir.

"I think I just broke a record for how fast I got him to sleep," Desmond grinned closing Desi's bedroom door.

"You might be right. I hate to admit it but maybe you do have the magic touch," Justina laughed.

"You mentioned you have a hair appointment, but do you have time for a drink before you go?"

"Sure." Justina welcomed the drink invite.

"Great, I'll try not to make it too strong," he remarked, guiding Justina to the kitchen. But they made a detour when the doorbell rang. "Who could that be?" Desmond wondered out loud, as Justina trailed close behind him.

"Hey!" Dominique beamed, holding their daughter in her arms. "I'm sorry, I didn't realize you had company," she said noticing Justina lurking in the back.

"Come in," he said warily. "I thought you were bringing Chloe over tomorrow?" Desmond was skeptical about the popup visit.

"Really...I thought I was supposed to bring her over on Thursday."

"Yeah, you are, but today is Wednesday."

Dominique gave a forced dumbfounded look. "Oh goodness, I'm so sorry! I can't believe I got the days confused. Being a new mother can have your brain frazzled. No worries, we'll come back tomorrow," Dominique said meekly.

"You don't have to do that," Desmond said placing Chloe in his arms. "She looks so adorable while sleeping."

"She really does." While Desmond was gushing over his daughter, Dominique used the opportunity to scoot closer to him. In Dominique's mind this was a win-win for her, she was bonding with her baby daddy and driving Justina crazy at the same damn time.

"I better get going," Justina said grabbing

her purse off the sofa. "I'm already running late for my hair appointment," she lied ready to get the fuck out of Desmond's house.

"I'll walk you out," Desmond said, about to hand Chloe back to Dominique.

"That's okay!" Justina was already out the door. "I'll call you later on to check on Desi."

"I hope Justina didn't rush out because of me." Dominique put on her best naïve tone, but Desmond knew better.

"That's exactly why she left, but you're already aware of this since the reason Justina divorced me in the first place is because of you," he said abruptly.

Desmond went and sat down on the sofa, cradling his daughter, who was only a few months old. She reminded him of a delicate baby doll that could easily be broken, so he was protective of her. Although it tore Desmond up losing his wife, once he held Chloe in his arms, he never regretted his daughter being born, even under the regrettable circumstances. He adored her and Dominique knew it, which is why she tried to use his adoration for the baby they shared together, to her advantage.

"I made a mistake and got the days confused. My goal wasn't to run Justina off. I had no idea she was even here," Dominique said, pulling a sad face. "It wasn't my intention to upset you. I just thought it would be nice if you spent some time with our daughter."

"You didn't upset me," Desmond sighed. "I love spending time with Chloe, even if I'm just holding her in my arms while she sleeps," he said lovingly staring at her.

"Even though she's just a baby, I know Chloe loves spending time with her daddy too. It's so beautiful watching you all bond." Dominique sat down next to Desmond on the sofa, placing her hand on his leg so effortlessly he didn't even detect she was running game. Dominique was well aware when she showed up at his front door unannounced, that this wasn't their scheduled visitation day to bring Chloe over. She also recognized Justina's car parked in the driveway and wanted to get her the fuck out of Desmond's house.

When Dominique discovered she was pregnant with Desmond's baby, she couldn't believe her luck. He was the biggest lick she could possibly hit. Dominique could have never imagined their one night of passion while being held hostage in the basement by her then ex-boyfriend Juan, would create her greatest blessing. She felt she was already winning by being the mother of

Desmond's child, but the gift that Justina handed her by filing for divorce was truly unexpected. The woman she believed was the only obstacle standing between her and the man she loved not only willingly gave him up, but also married another man. Dominique felt her pregnancy was the gift that kept on giving.

So, a couple months ago when Dominique first noticed Justina and not the nanny was co ming around, she realized her shit was in danger. She was aware Desmond was still in love with his ex-wife, but she figured that once he accepted Justina had moved on and was never coming back to him, in time they would end up back in bed together and eventually become a happy family. When Dominique did her popup visit today and saw Desmond and Justina together, she knew her dreams of becoming his wife was in jeopardy. There was no way she was going to sit back and allow that to happen. As far as Dominique was concerned, Justina had her opportunity to hold on to Desmond, but like the spoiled, self-entitled brat she was, because he betrayed her, she let him go, leaving the door wide open for her. Now that Dominique stepped through it, she would destroy anyone that tried to get in the way of her becoming the next Mrs. Desmond Blackwell.

Chapter Eleven

Elusive Expectations

"Supreme, stop trying to change my mind!" Precious stormed out the house that was Nico's secret hideaway shouting and marched through the front door of the home she shared with Supreme still doing the same shit. He allowed his wife to express herself without interrupting for the last hour but now it was his turn.

"Can I speak?" Supreme followed Precious to the kitchen, listening intently while she continued to justify why the truth needed to come out about Nico. The more she talked, Precious only bolstered his stance that they needed to wait.

"Fine...speak." Precious sat down on one of the turquoise velvet upholstered bar stools, behind the sprawling dark gray marble waterfall island. She appeared annoyed, glancing around the Arabic inspired designed grandeur kitchen with high ceilings, arches with wood detailing, and a sumptuous touch of blue that contrasted with the white walls and floors. There was a large contemporary bubble light that made a statement while keeping the open layout space feeling airy. Precious blatantly focused her attention on the light fixture, letting Supreme know she wasn't interested in hearing anything he had to say on this topic. She was angry with her husband. To the extent that typically this kitchen area put Precious in a relaxing mood, but not even all this luxury surrounding them, could calm her nerves.

"Are you even listening to what the fuck I'm tellin' you right now?" he asked harshly.

"Not really," Precious admitted offhandedly, tapping her almond shaped French manicure on the sleek white marble top.

"I'm sorry if this is boring you," Supreme mocked, but this isn't about you. It's about saving Nico's life."

"Excuse me! What the hell are you insinuating right now?"

"You know that Maverick has a target on Genesis' back and anyone he deems close to him. If word got out that Nico survived his injuries and wasn't dead, his priority would be to finish him off," Supreme barked.

"As if Aaliyah would ever put Nico in danger. She deserves to know her father is alive!"

"The more people who know the truth, the greater the risks grow for Nico. Like you hiring that private investigator who found the house where Nico is staying. Trust and believe he is going to run his mouth to somebody, and if he found the house, somebody else can too. This ain't about you being in your feelings because you were kept in the dark regarding Nico!"

"Fuck you, Supreme! You damn right I was in my feelings. How dare you keep a secret like that from me!"

"It wasn't my secret to tell," he refuted. "What about that don't you understand. You think I wanted to carry this burden? Why tha fuck do you think I didn't show up to Nico's homegoing celebration. Watching everyone mourn for a man I knew was alive. Why do you think I've isolated myself away from you and everyone else!" he exclaimed.

"Then why do it?!" Precious screamed back.

"Because it's what Nico wanted, *and* it was the right thing to do. That's a fact, now deal with it." Supreme demanded, bolting from what had become a dead-end conversation.

The open back chainmail silver mini dress was giving the come-hither affect Aaliyah wanted to lure Gabriel Cattaneo into her baited trap. She stared at her reflection in the full-length mirror pleased with her appearance. She put on another layer of gloss wanting her lips to have a super wet look. "Perfect." Aaliyah smiled widely.

"Wow! Girl, you look amazing!" Angel gushed when she entered the bathroom in the hotel suite the sisters were sharing. "Gabriel won't be able to resist you," she said pleased with how Aaliyah was the replica of walking temptation.

"I'm feeling extremely optimistic myself," Aaliyah nodded, fluffing out her hair. "And I must say, this dress you picked out is fuckin' amazing. It fits like you had it tailored for my body. Very impressive," she said with a flash of glimmer in her eyes.

"Thank you...thank you," Angel did a playful

bow and waved her hand. "I'm being silly right now but let's get serious for a moment," she said sitting on top the sink counter next to where Aaliyah was standing. "Tell me the truth...do you have any reservations about moving forward with this?"

Aaliyah put her hands on Angel's shoulders, staring directly in her eyes. "No and stop worrying...I got this."

"I will have eyes on you at all times. Inside the club and outside. The guy who manages the spot is going to introduce you to Gabriel because he is always surrounded by bodyguards. Once he makes the introduction, it's all on you. If you get uncomfortable or scared at any time, promise me you'll bolt. Promise me, Aaliyah," Angel insisted.

"Promise," Aaliyah said hugging her sister. "Now come on, we can't be late to the party!"

"Nico, can I get you anything before I turn in for the night?" Kyra asked walking over to the sitting area where he was watching television.

"No, I'm good."

"Well, if you decide you want something to eat before bed, Valerie is still up. See you in the morning. Goodnight."

"Thank you and goodnight," Nico said then deciding he needed to speak with her before she went to bed. "Kyra!" He called out, stopping her from leaving.

"Yes."

"I meant to speak with you earlier, but I've had a lot on my mind," Nico said gripping the wheels of the chair with his hands thrusting forward towards Kyra.

"What is it?"

"I wanted to apologize for what happened the other day with Precious."

"There's no need for you to apologize. What happened wasn't your fault," Kyra said. "But I appreciate you caring."

"I do care. Don't ever doubt it. You've been by my side since I was released from the hospital. You've done a great deal for me. I may not be walking yet, but you deserve all the credit for the progress I've made so far."

"I don't deserve all the credit. Your determination has played a major part. And we can't forget how stubborn you are," Kyra laughed. "How many times have I told you that's enough when doing foot drop exercises, but you refuse to listen. You won't even use the electric wheelchair

Supreme got for you. You insist on the manu-
al one because you said it's building up your
strength faster."

"I'm tryna get out this wheelchair, not stay
in it. I don't want to get comfortable to the point
that I become content getting around using a
joystick," Nico frowned irately. "And it's not stub-
bornness it's motivation."

"Motivated to get back to your previous life?"
Kyra questioned.

"To a degree but most importantly, I miss my
daughters. I love them both, but one came into
my life when she was grown. I was trying to make
up for lost time," Nico paused with a heavy heart.
"Then we were ripped apart. I want to get back
to them, but not like this." There was a significant
amount of somberness in his tone.

"Does part of the motivation have anything
to do with the woman who showed up accusing
me of having an affair with her husband? She demanded I answer questions about my relationship with him, but when she saw you, none of
that mattered."

"We share a long history," Nico disclosed.

"It's obvious the two of you are extremely
close."

"We are. We also have a daughter together."

"Is that the reason she's so territorial when it comes to you? I realize she's married, but she strikes me as the type that wouldn't let something like a marriage license stop her from doing what she wants."

"Precious can come across a bit aggressive but..."

"That's an understatement," Kyra interrupted. "I was thinking more like volatile."

"She has her ways, but Precious also has a big heart."

"Are you in love with her?" Kyra hoped her candid question did not offend Nico. "Am I being too intrusive? I'll admit being around you every day, I've gotten comfortable and feel that we can discuss just about anything. But if I've crossed the line, please let me know."

"No, I'm not offended, and you haven't crossed the line. You've seen me helpless and at my most vulnerable, so I get it."

"I've seen you physically helpless and vulnerable but people, especially men, tend to be much more guarded when it comes to their heart," Kyra stated with certainty. Kyra's assessment on this particular matter was ultraprecise. Even at his most vulnerable, Nico had always remained reserved with what he shared with her. Kyra was his nurse, caretaker and in a lot of ways, he considered her a confidante. But she knew very little about the actual man, Nico Carter.

Kyra had been a Nurse Practitioner for a few years at Houston Methodist when she decided a change of scenery was needed. Although she loved caring for patients, the toll of an increased workload, longer shifts, due in part to a nursing shortage had led to burnout. Adding to the stress was the fact there was too much time devoted to paperwork and electronic health records. Kyra chose her career path because it was challenging, and it would give her the opportunity to make a positive difference in her patients' lives on a daily basis. But she had been spending too much time on unnecessary paperwork and not enough time with her patients. Her job had become unfulfilling. She also wanted to live closer to her mother, who resided in New York. She was an only child, and after her father died unexpectedly a few years ago, Kyra felt in a lot of ways they only had each other.

A doctor who Kyra worked closely with at Houston Methodist hospital, knew she was considering a move to New York. So, when a doctor who remained a friend after they attended the same medical residency program mentioned one of his patients would need a highly skilled nurse, who could live with him, he immediately thought of Kyra. She jumped at the opportunity and took the first available flight to New York for an interview. First, she met with the doctor, then Supreme and finally Nico. After a rigorous interview process, they all agreed she was the perfect fit, which thrilled Kyra. This was her dream job—to be able to focus all the nursing skills she acquired over the years on an individual patient, to help him reach his health goals. Nico proved to be Kyra's most challenging patient but also the most rewarding.

Chapter 12

Affairs Of The Heart

Cosmo Terrace near Rittenhouse Square was the perfect lush outdoor lounging and garden dining space. The open-air eatery had floor-to-ceiling Persian ironwood trees surrounded by cool brick and stone walls, modern art, trickling fountains and a fire pit which created what resembled a scenic hideaway.

Caleb and Shiffon sat under a veranda, draped with hanging strings of white lights, filled with potted shrubs and eye pleasing mint green chairs. He was eating traditional Italian pasta and she had a tasty seafood dish.

"I have to come back here again because this food was delicious," Shiffon said sipping on sparkling rose.

"Yeah, Floyd loved this spot too," Caleb said as his mind drifted away, becoming engrossed in his own thoughts.

"I know Floyd's death hit you hard. A while back you mentioned your brother's girlfriend had something to do with it. Did anything come of that?"

"Yeah, she's dead."

"Wait...what?" Shiffon was stunned by the news. "It wasn't..."

"No." Caleb shook his head interrupting Shiffon, knowing what she was about to ask. "I had nothing to do wit' that shit but I don't give a fuck 'bout the bitch being dead either."

"I feel you. There are some people who are better off dead," Shiffon justified.

"With the line of business you in, you would know," Caleb said cracking a smile.

"Cute...very cute."

"I was surprised when you reached out to me saying you were in town. I thought you weren't going back to work for at least a couple weeks."

"Initially that was the plan. But umm, I got a

job offer that's paying extremely well. Since my mom and brother are both good, I decided to fly in and meet with the potential client. But before I took the job, I wanted to make sure you didn't need my services. I don't like to start a job and not finish it," Shiffon established.

"You always been 'bout yo' business," Caleb recognized. "And I respect that. I really didn't wanna say nothin' over the phone, plus I wanted to get confirmation, which I got earlier today."

"Confirmation about what?"

"Maverick is done," Caleb announced.

"Are you sure?" Shiffon asked fidgeting around her neck. Whenever she felt a bit anxious, she had a habit of fondling the necklace she wore that had a heart locket with a picture of her and her little brother. She typically never took it off and wondered if she left the necklace at the hotel. Shiffon thought of the locket as a good luck charm, and with her line of business, she needed all the luck she could get.

"Positive. They caught that nigga in some ultra-exclusive resort in Fiji. You gotta give that muthafucka credit, he knew how to live good," Caleb chuckled. "He went out blazin' too 'cause he murked one of them hitters before they finally put him to rest."

"So, Maverick is dead?" Shiffon lowered her voice and asked, even though she knew what Caleb meant by the term done.

"Yep. He had some chick wit' him too. Unfortunately, she was in the wrong place at the wrong time and caught them bullets with him."

"Wow, it's hard to believe he's done. Maverick has been on our radar for so long. I'm disappointed it wasn't me that got the job done. Damn, I kinda feel like a failure," Shiffon joked.

"Yeah right, failure my ass!" Caleb laughed. "But nah you shouldn't. If it makes you feel any better, it was some mob hitters that got him."

"Are you serious? Do I have new competition for my line of work? I mean, I didn't know the mob stepped in and took out people that hadn't crossed them directly."

"Nope, no worries on that front. From my understanding, Genesis called in a favor with the head of a major crime family," Caleb divulged.

"Then I guess you were right, no need for me to feel like a failure. Genesis got some elite gangsters to handle shit."

"That's why he the boss. But seriously, glad we can put that shit in the rearview mirror. I was tired of lookin' over my shoulder. He had bodies droppin' everywhere. My man Floyd dead 'cause of Maverick. I wanted my pound of flesh. It was time for that nigga to go. At this point, I didn't care who killed him, as long as the shit got done," Caleb spit.

"I get it, I really do." Shiffon reached across the table and held Caleb's hands. Floyd's murder continued to weigh heavy on his heart. She didn't know when or if Caleb would ever get over the loss of his best friend. His pain ran deep.

Mia watched from a short distance while Shiffon consoled Caleb. She had been fixated on the pair since they sat down at the upscale bistro. *You claimed you had business to handle but here you are with that bitch! How dare you leave me alone to come be with her. She doesn't deserve you, Caleb. Shiffon will never love you the way I do,* Mia thought to herself consumed with rage. After Caleb left his apartment, Mia made the decision to follow him. Once she realized he was with Shiffon, she became immersed in her paranoia. Imagining they were involved in a passionate love affair behind her back. Shiffon was another obstacle keeping her and Caleb apart. She made up her mind that Shiffon had to go. Mia would erase her from their lives the exact same way she permanently deleted her sister.

"Babe, I'm back!" Shiffon called out when she entered their hotel room. He wasn't in the sitting area, so she went and checked the bedroom. "There you are," she smiled when she saw Maverick closing the glass door to the hotel room balcony.

"I didn't realize you were back. How long have you been here?" he asked wrapping his arms around Shiffon's waist and pulling her close for a kiss.

"Just walked in. I called out for you, but I guess you didn't hear me."

"Yeah, I was outside on a call. I came back in because it was mad windy out there. How did things go with Caleb...did you find out anything?"

"It worked. They think you're dead."

"Are you sure?"

"Positive. Caleb said that you were killed in Fiji, and you were with a woman, who was also shot and killed," Shiffon informed him.

"Did you find out who the shooters were?"

"I did. Genesis called in a favor with some mob boss. He sent in his shooters."

"Get tha fuck outta here." Maverick was pacing the floor with a contorted frown on his face. "This nigga got mob hitters targeting me. I guess it's a good thing, they think I'm dead," he mocked.

"Definitely, because as irresistible as you are, I don't think those hitters would fall in love with you and be unable to finish the job they were hired to do," Shiffon teased. She was trying to lighten the mood, because there was no denying Maverick's fury.

"They would still be huntin' me down if Micah and the woman with him hadn't been there. That nigga was my day one and now he dead too." Maverick pounded his fist against the wall.

Shiffon inhaled deeply knowing there was nothing she could say that would ease Maverick's pain. She was still shaken from their close encounter with death in Fiji. When gunshots started ringing through the bungalow, Shiffon and Maverick went through a bathroom that connected to the bedroom where Micah was staying. When they entered the room, they thought Micah was in a deep sleep, but when Maverick started to shake his chest to wake him up, his hands were covered in blood. That's when he also noticed a woman lying beside Micah, her body riddled with bullets. The sheets soaked in blood. Both were dead.

They went into survivor mode. Maverick

exchanged ammo with the hitters while Shiffon set the stage to make it appear that Micah's dead body was Maverick, since they knew he was the one they came for. Luckily most of Micah's personal belongings was at the hotel room he was sharing with Cam, so Shiffon didn't have to put in an exorbitant amount of work to alter the scene. But with bullets coming from every direction, up until the very moment they made their escape, Shiffon felt like she was on the brink of death.

"Babe, I think we should get out of Philly and lay low until all this craziness die down," Shiffon suggested.

"I need you to do one more thing for me before we go." Maverick stated regaining his composure.

"Sure, what is it?"

"That call I was just on; I received some interesting information."

"Okay, what information and what do you need me to do with it?" Shiffon was ready to get the hell out of Philly and the surrounding areas. The quicker she could make good on what Maverick wanted her to do, the quicker they could leave town.

"Nico Carter didn't die after all. He is alive."

"But they had a funeral and everything for

him?" she was stunned. The twist and turns kept coming.

"Smoke and mirrors. It explains why the nigga was supposedly cremated. Genesis wanted it to appear that nigga was dead, but they got him stashed and I need to know where."

"Why? This shit is over they think you dead. It's horrible what happened to Micah and the woman that was with him, but the mob hit turned out to be a gift for you."

"Fuck that! You know how many of my men are in a grave because of Genesis. Killin' Nico was a major win, and that win will be mine!" Maverick roared.

"Not sure how I can help." Shiffon threw her hands up not wanting any part of this.

"Meet up wit' that nigga Caleb again. He run his mouth a lot when he's around you. Find out where Genesis got his man stashed at."

"No."

Maverick's eyebrows narrowed. "I don't think I heard you correctly. Surely you didn't use the word no."

"Yes, I did. I already went to Caleb to find out who was behind the hit and if they believed you were dead or alive. I'm not going back a second time to pick his brain about Nico."

"Why tha fuck not? I know that nigga soft on you, are you soft on him too?" Maverick pressed Shiffon for an answer.

"No, I'm not soft on Caleb but he's already been through enough. His best friend is dead behind this war between you and Genesis."

"That nigga know how the game go. Casualties are part of warfare. Ain't nobody immune."

"I will not play a role in leading you to Nico Carter. If you want Nico dead, you'll have to find him yourself, because I won't help. I'm done wit' this shit!"

"Shiffon, you can't be on the fence. You gon' have to pick a side and stand by it."

"What the fuck do you think I did when I got on that plane with you. Or going to Caleb, someone I consider a friend and runnin' bullshit on him so he could tell me what I needed to know, so I could then deliver that information to you. I'm done jumpin' out the window to get you information on Genesis and his crew. You survived them. It's time for us to escape the chaos and start our lives over somewhere else."

Maverick and Shiffon were now entering their own war against each other. She felt she had given up everything for him, but he felt she hadn't given up enough. They reached an impasse and depending on which emotion was stronger—love or hatred, would determine how their forbidden love affair would end.

Chapter 13

No Love In The Club

"Baby, you sure you don't wanna come to the club with me?" Amir asked Justina one last time, hoping he could change her mind. "We won't be there long. I just have to conduct a little business, then we can have a drink and leave."

"Not tonight," she again declined. "Desi is coming home tomorrow, so I need to be well rested. The older he gets the more active," Justina smiled.

"Yeah, my lil' guy is definitely a handful." Amir stated proudly. "He hella funny too. His personality is getting bigger and bigger."

"Sure is. It's not the same when Desi isn't here with us. He lights up the place when he's home."

"What time is Maria bringing Desi home tomorrow?" Amir questioned putting on his ivory knit Gucci Boutique intarsia label polo shirt with blue and red stripes contrasted with shiny metal buttons. He was going for a casual yet clean pristine look. The intrinsic vintage feel of the polo top mixed with some Hollywood glamour allowed Amir to pull the look off effortlessly.

"Maria needed me to drop Desi off, so I figured I'd pick him up too," Justina said aimlessly flipping through some random magazine.

"I can pick Desi up," Amir said stepping out his closet into the hallway. He could see Justina sitting comfortably on the velvet upholstery left arm curved back chaise lounge, standing atop gold stainless steel legs.

"That's okay, I don't mind. He's been gone for over a week. I'm looking forward to picking Desi up."

"Maybe we can pick him up together," Amir suggested. "Depending what time I finish my lunch meeting tomorrow."

"Sure, just let me know," Justina turned

around and said to Amir who was still standing in the hallway.

"Will do." Amir stared at his wife for a few more seconds before stepping back into his custom walk-in closet. He opened the glass door on the closet hutch to retrieve one of the watches off the shelf from his extensive collection. While securing the timepiece around his wrist, Amir realized his mistrust was getting the best of him, and he was rattled.

When Amir proposed to Justina, he didn't fool himself into believing she was completely over Desmond. They were still married and the only reason she filed for divorce was because of his infidelity. But once they exchanged vows and became one, he trusted she would be completely devoted to keeping their family intact. There was no denying they shared a complex history, but there was a tremendous amount of love and more importantly, they created a son together which he believed formed an unbreakable bond between them. But when Justina mentioned she had dropped Desi off and was picking him up, his intuition told him Desmond continued to have an emotional hold on his wife. He had no intention of losing his family. Amir was devoted to taking the necessary steps to keep the former lovers apart until Justina was no longer in love with Desmond.

Once Aaliyah arrived at the nightclub, she made a stop in the restroom to make sure her hair, makeup and outfit was still on point. Pleased with the visuals, she went right into work mode. She distanced herself from everyone, so she could scope out her surroundings. Although Aaliyah knew the club's manager would be making a formal introduction, she wanted to observe the way Gabriel Cattaneo moved beforehand.

Not surprisingly, Gabriel had one of the premier booths in the club. It was positioned in the center on the upper level, which allowed him to be seen by all and to also keep everyone else in his view. As Angel had already said, he kept several bodyguards within his reach. The best way to take him out would be to get him alone, and that would require Aaliyah to be able to seduce a man she loathed.

"A'ight bitch, let's do this," Aaliyah said out loud, hyping herself up to make her move. As she began to maneuver through the club, *Late At Night* by Roddy Ricch came on. She didn't know if it was because that song always had a way of making her feel sexy, or a buzz from the couple glasses of champagne she drank before arriving at the club was creeping in, but at the last-minute Aaliyah decided to slightly change up her game plan.

Aaliyah noticed this one particular guy who was sitting at a table near Gabriel's booth, had zoomed in on her while she was walking towards the stairs. She chose to use that to her advantage. She slowly sauntered up the sleek spiral staircase, gripping the curved glass handrail and stainless-steel stringers. Aaliyah stopped midway on the marble steps to lock eyes with the cute guy she planned to use as a prop. The thin flexible LED invisible stripes inserted below the handrail and into the stringers had Aaliyah glowing under the bright lights like she was the star of the show. By the time she reached the top of the stairs, the cute guy was waiting for her.

"You are gorgeous," he said extending his hand as if to help her step off the last stair.

"Thank you."

"Come sit down and have a drink with me."

"You sure your friends won't mind?" she asked looking over at the two other guys sitting down.

"That's my table, so you good," he assured her. "Will you join me?"

"I suppose," Aaliyah said with a coy smile. When she took a seat, from the corner of her eye she saw Gabriel staring in her direction. She knew she'd caught his attention, now she just had to keep it. With the bottles of champagne poppin' and the music blasting it wasn't hard. When the DJ dropped *Top Notch* and City Girls verse came on, Aaliyah was ready to begin her sexual seduction performance.

I just got my hair did, then shit on hoes like it's a hobby
Every bitch that hate on me got an ugly face and a botched body
I ain't going there, that's an opp party
I'm a bad bitch, I'm a Black Barbie
Any nigga I call bro, they fuck bitches and catch bodies
Ain't no more play time, they like cut the lights, it's daytime
I told my niggas he betta act right
'Cause to fuck with me, it's a wait line
Bitch better move when I come through
Fly bitches need privacy
Shy niggas say hi to me

Broke boys say bye to me
Period...

Amir left out the back office after finishing up his business meeting with Max, the club owner. Before leaving he stopped at the bar for a drink and became distracted when he glanced up and noticed a familiar silhouette gyrating seductively to the music. When the woman turned around, he was stunned to see it was Aaliyah. A tall, well-built man was standing behind her with his hands on her hips, admiring the way she was moving her body. An unexpected surge of jealousy shot through Amir. He had an impulse to rush up the stairs and grab Aaliyah, but he stopped himself. Not only was she not his woman he had a wife at home. *Let me get the fuck outta here,* Amir thought to himself ready to leave until he was stopped by the manager.

"Max needs to speak with you again before you go," the manager told Amir who was finishing up his drink.

"Is he still in his office?" Amir wanted to confirm.

"Yep."

"Cool." Amir put his glass down and headed back to Max's office.

Aaliyah pretended not to see Amir standing by the bar staring at her. Once she became aware of his presence, she upped the ante, not only using her prop to lure Gabriel into her trap, but to also send Amir into a jealous rage. She had begun swaying her hips harder, and while the cute guy stood behind her, she utilized his hands to make love to the curves on her body. He was turning out to be the perfect prop. He was good looking enough for other men to see him as viable competition and sexy enough for her not to mind his hands being all over her. Aaliyah could feel him getting a rise, which didn't bother her if she accomplished what she intended. So, you can imagine the blow to her ego when Amir didn't storm the table and drag her out the club. Instead, he finished his drink and walked away.

Fuck you Amir! I should've known you would walk away instead of fighting for me...for us. It's probably for the best. I can't lose sight of the reason I'm here in the first place—to get Gabriel, Aaliyah thought to herself glancing up, feeling a pair of eyes burning a hole through her dress. It was Gabriel. Unlike Amir, he didn't run away. He motioned his hand for Aaliyah to come to him.

Bingo!

"Excuse me for a second. I need to speak with a friend of mine," Aaliyah whispered in the guy's ear.

"Don't go," he said holding on to her hand.

"I promise, I'll be right back," Aaliyah lied and said. If everything went the way she hoped, she would be leaving the club with Gabriel Cattaneo.

Gabriel's bodyguards stepped to the side allowing Aaliyah to get near him. He greeted her with one of those villainous smiles that Aaliyah knew he thought made him appear enthralling.

"You're fuckin' hot," Gabriel stated, squeezing her upper thigh crudely. "I'm Gabriel. What's your name, gorgeous?"

"Aaliyah."

"Aaliyah, I've never seen you in here before. Do you live in Miami or are you visiting?"

"Visiting."

"You can't be visiting with that man you were dancing with."

"You're right. I just met him at the club tonight."

"Are you a working girl?"

"Excuse me?" Aaliyah giggled.

"Are you selling pussy? You said you just met that man tonight, but he had his hands all over you while dancing. He was pretty much dry fucking you on the floor."

"Do I look like a prostitute to you?"

"A high end one. Don't be offended. Your shoes, that dress you're wearing. Your makeup, hair, everything about you looks first class...very expensive and you're beautiful. Type of woman I like." Gabriel pressed down on Aaliyah's thigh again.

"I'm not a prostitute, high end call girl or an escort. None of that."

"Well how about you be one tonight. I pay extremely well." Gabriel flashed what appeared to be an endless amount of one-hundred-dollar bills.

"I might be game," Aaliyah teased, sliding her finger across his lips.

"Come with me," he demanded yanking her arm, pulling Aaliyah off the couch. Two of Gabriel's bodyguards were trailing right behind them.

"Where are we going?" Aaliyah asked doing her best not to seem bothered. She debated if she should send Angel a text, but she convinced herself she could handle whatever Gabriel threw her way, and as of now, he wasn't a threat.

"We're going to have a little fun before leaving," Gabriel said keeping a firm grip on Aaliyah's arm, leading her to the men's restroom. "Don't let anyone come in," he told his bodyguards who were posted outside the door.

Once behind closed doors, Gabriel wasted no time snorting several lines of coke off the bathroom sink counter. He also pulled out a few pills from his pocket but instead of swallowing them, he opened the capsules and snorted the powder. Aaliyah knew this was her clue to exit immediately but two things were stopping her. She felt she may never get another opportunity to get this close to Gabriel, but she was also feeling somewhat trapped in the bathroom.

"Where the fuck do you think you going?" Gabriel shouted when he noticed Aaliyah tiptoe-ing away.

"I'll be right back. I forgot my purse upstairs and I need to go get it."

"That shit can wait," he barked yanking Aali-yah towards him. "Come take a hit."

Demons were all in his eyes, making Aaliyah be cautious with her approach. "No thank you," she said politely.

"That wasn't a fuckin' question!" Gabriel placed his hand around the back of Aaliyah's neck pushing her face down on the counter in the cocaine.

"Get off me!" Aaliyah screamed.

"Boss is everything okay in here?" one of Gabriel's bodyguards opened the bathroom door to check on him after hearing the commotion.

"Close the fuckin' door and don't come back in here or else!" Gabriel threatened.

"Help!" Aaliyah was barely able to get the word out because Gabriel covered her mouth, suppressing her pleas.

"My men are guarding the door, so nobody is coming for you," he said taunting Aaliyah. "Now snort that coke. You'll enjoy this dick I'm about to shove up in you a lot more if you're high." Gabriel gave a sinister laugh.

Aaliyah felt helpless. No matter how hard she tried to fight back she was no match for Gabriel. *Dear God, please don't let me get raped! Why didn't I text Angel when I had the chance? I'm so stupid!* Aaliyah thought, yelling to herself. She commenced to panicking when the inevitable set in, she was about to get raped in the men's restroom. Tears were flooding Aaliyah's face as she braced herself for what was about to happen next.

"You sick fuck...I should kill you." Amir quietly seethed in Gabriel's ear holding him in a rear naked choke. He tried to struggle to get out the hold, but the effectiveness had begun once Amir slid his arm around Gabriel's neck and got it locked in. Now there was nothing Gabriel could do to get out the chokehold in time.

Amir applied constant pressure on Gabriel's neck, compressing his windpipe. He continued to squeeze his arms tight, applying additional pressure to the carotid arteries cutting off blood flow to his brain. Amir was causing deadly consequences because he had cut off Gabriel's ability to expand his lungs and take in air while at the same time cutting off the blood flow to the brain. Within six to nine seconds, he was rendered unconscious. He faded out and his body went limp. At this point Amir should've released the choke because at the twenty second mark is when brain damage starts and can easily become permanent if prevention tactics aren't implemented. But Amir's fury caused him to black out. Twenty seconds became sixty and Gabriel began to turn blue in the face. He seemed to lose track of time, soon minutes passed, and Amir had not let go. It was seeing Aaliyah's disheveled hair, smeared makeup and her tears, which had not stopped flowing that brought him out of his haze. Amir released Gabriel's dead body from his grasp and let out a heavy sigh.

"Amir, you saved me," Aaliyah sobbed falling into his arms. "Don't ever leave me." She closed her eyes wanting to stay in Amir's embrace forever.

"I'm not going anywhere," Amir assured Aaliyah, staring down at the man he just killed, thinking the muthafucka got exactly what he deserved.

Chapter Fourteen

Broken Alliance

"Good morning." Precious gave her best pleasant smile when Kyra opened the door. "I'm here to see Nico. I'm sure he told you he was expecting me."

"Yes, he did. Come in." Kyra cut her eyes at Precious, stepping to the side to allow her to come through. "You're a bit early."

"I am, but he won't mind."

"Nico is out by the pool with his physical therapists. They'll be done in about an hour," Kyra informed Precious, who was standing in the foyer with her arms folded like this was her house.

"I'll wait. I'm in no rush."

"Fine. I'm sure you'll have no problem making yourself at home," Kyra said walking off.

"Where are you headed?" she asked.

"Out back," Kyra answered shortly.

"I'll join you." Precious followed Kyra to the covered patio and sat down on one of the lounge chairs. It gave the ladies a direct view of Nico, who was in the pool with his physical therapists. Precious could see his intense workouts was paying off. "Nico appears to be making exceptional progress."

"Yes, he is. I've never had a patient with more determination than him." Kyra did not try to hide her admiration for Nico and Precious took notice.

"It's obvious you're very fond of Nico."

"Back at you," Kyra reciprocated. "How does your husband feel about that?"

"That's none of your business but since I falsely accused you of being his mistress, I'll play nice and answer your question. My husband understands that I will always have love for Nico and be concerned about his wellbeing. Since we're asking questions and answering them truthfully—answer this, does Nico know you're in love with him?"

"Excuse me?" Kyra stammered with her response. That was not the question she was expecting. "Not sure where that came from."

"I recognize that look of love and you have it bad for Nico. I just don't want you to get your feelings hurt."

"Oh, so are you concerned for me, or do you think I wouldn't appeal to a man like Nico because I'm not a glamour girl like you," Kyra commented, scrutinizing the white cotton dress from Dior that Precious was wearing. It flowed around her on the breezy day, ending midway down her calves. The night gown style dress was fringed around the decolletage with scalloped lace and again at the high waist above the loose wide skirt. She accessorized the sundress with a Prada tote, a pair of gold-tinted reflective aviator sunglasses, and strappy platform high heel sandals. Around her neck was an array of dainty butterfly queen layered gold necklaces with diamond details. Precious had her hair up in a casual bun, displaying her well-defined collarbone. To Precious this was her effortless chic attire not glamour.

"Well, I'm not a girl, I'm a grown woman as you can clearly see," Precious sniped. "But it has nothing to do with that. And based on your comment, evidently, Nico mentioned the long history we share."

"He did and that you all have a daughter together. But he didn't go into any details and honestly, I don't want to know."

"You should. The more you understand Nico's past, the more you'll understand who he is as a man. Because he is complicated, and he's driven. His determination has nothing to do with him getting shot and wanting to recover from his surgery. It's because Nico is a survivor. He's been fighting his entire life and a bullet won't stop him. Do you really want to be in love with a man like that? Because you will never come first in his life."

"I see you're doing your best to scare me away. But I've been through my own struggles, so I don't scare easily. I can handle anything that might happen between me and Nico, so I'm not worried at all," she stated confidently.

"Then I guess you're not as smart as I thought you were," Precious scoffed.

"After our conversation, I think we can agree on two things; your relationship with your husband is none of my business, and my relationship with Nico is none of yours. Now excuse me, I have a patient to tend to."

"Genesis, thank you for coming to meet with me here at my home," Silvano said puffing on his signature cigar. "Can I get you anything while we wait for dinner to be served?"

"No, I'm good. I appreciate the invite for dinner. This is the first time I've been to your home, and you didn't disappoint. It's exactly what I would expect from you," Genesis remarked eyeing an estate that many would consider a masterpiece.

The palatial 16,000 square feet colonial stone manor with panoramic western views in Alpine, New Jersey was a perfect representation of how Silvano Cattaneo wanted his guests to view him—that this was his kingdom, and he was the king. The two-story marble entry foyer with an iron bridal staircase and six large reception rooms flooded with light were perfect for the grand scale entertaining that Silvano loved to do. The large chef's kitchen opened to a stone terrace leading to a covered loggia. There was a huge primary bedroom suite on the second level with a fireplace, two wardrobe rooms, and onyx bathroom. There were four additional bedrooms suites and an enormous wood paneled studio loft. The lower level of his mansion had a wet bar, theater, gym, library, with an indoor cabana. The bright solarium with walls of windows opened to a private heavily landscaped oasis, featuring a gazebo overlooking a picturesque stream, heated pool with a spa.

"When I purchased this place, I envisioned it being filled with my sons, their wives and my grandchildren. But they didn't share my vision," Silvano laughed. "Now, I live in this fuckin' huge house pretty much alone. Luckily, I enjoy throwing spectacular parties all year round. When I have my next one, you must attend Genesis," he insisted.

"I will be here," he nodded in agreement.

"Thank you, my friend," Silvano said shaking the ice in his glass of bourbon. "I'm assuming I can refer to you again as my friend...correct? I mean, I delivered to you what you wanted...yes."

"Yes, you did, and I'm grateful to you because of it. For well over a year, this man had become a serious problem for me. Now, for the first time in months, I feel that I can focus my energy on business instead of constantly worrying that my family is in danger," Genesis said relishing in his relief.

"I feel fortunate I was able to help. As you stated before and you were correct, I owed you. Can we agree my debt has been fulfilled?"

"Yes, we can."

"Good!" Silvano clapped his hands together. "Now that we've gotten that out the way, we can move forward to what I would like to discuss."

"Which is?"

"Genesis, I told you I had my own motivation for helping you out. I want us to work together again. Your strong ties to the DC, Charlotte, Philadelphia and Atlanta markets would bring in the revenue my family has been deficient. We can't seem to break meaningful ground in those areas. I'll supply you with the best product and give you a substantial break on pricing. We will make a shitload of money together. It will feel like old times...in a good way," Silvano smiled.

"I never had a problem doing business with you, Silvano, but your son is a different story. What if he decides to once again renege on our agreement?"

"Stop right there." Silvano put his hand up in the name of peace. "I give you, my word. Gabriel will not interfere with our business arrangement. In fact, he will be the go-to person. Because if he messes up, he has been warned, I will cut him off."

"Really?" Genesis wasn't quite sold on what Silvano was selling.

"Yes. My son has been fuckin' up a great deal lately. Several months ago, he had someone killed that he knew was off limits. I had to do a lot of cleaning up because of Gabriel's reckless decision. I will not tolerate such poor judgement again," Silvano promised.

"I'm taking you at your word, Silvano. We can work together on this. I will have my son be the point person on my end. He deals directly with the connects in each of the locations you mentioned. When you're ready, we can set up a time and place for them to meet."

"I'm ready now!" Silvano smacked his leg, releasing a heavy bellow. "You know when it comes to business, I prefer not to delay."

"I do remember," Genesis nodded.

"Does your son live in New York or in the surrounding area? I can have Gabriel meet him here."

"Amir lives in Miami. But if it's more convenient for him to come here, that won't be a problem."

"My friend, this new business venture is meant to be. My son also lives in Miami. He's addicted to that nightlife scene." Silvano frowned his face. "Putting him to work at these locations will force him to think about more than sticking his dick in new pussy all the time."

"You mean that's what you hope," Genesis cracked.

"Yes, it is a strong hope. I assume you have the same problems with your own son, so you can relate."

"Amir is a married man with a beautiful wife and son."

"That means you're a grandfather."

"Yes, I am a very proud grandfather."

"You lucky sonofabitch," Silvano shook his head. "I've begged Gabriel to stay the fuck out the clubs and find a good woman to marry...give me some grandkids. He won't listen," he complained throwing his arms up. "Soon, if he doesn't settle down, I'll have to threaten him."

"I feel you. I'm sure you'll figure out how to get what you want from your son. In the meantime, I'll speak with Amir and let him know he'll be linking up with Gabriel in the very near future."

"Wonderful my friend," Silvano said as he and Genesis shook hands. "We shall make a massive amount of money together. Now let's go eat! We have lots to celebrate."

Chapter Fifteen

Distress Signal

"Are you tired of me showing up every day to visit you yet?" Precious laughed while pushing Nico in his wheelchair on a pathway right behind his backyard, which led to a nature trail that surrounded a sprawling botanical garden.

"Not yet but if you keep bossing the staff around, they might demand you be permanently barred."

"I'm not bossy," Precious played perplexed. "I just want to make sure everyone is doing their part to get you back to one hundred percent."

"They are. I'm not the easiest person to please," Nico acknowledged, "But they've all been phenomenal, especially Kyra."

"You do know she's in love with you, Kyra that is," Precious stated without dubiety.

"According to you every woman in that house is in love with me," Nico chuckled.

"No, I said they were enamored with you, which is true. Kyra is in love with you. There's a difference." Precious stopped pushing Nico's wheelchair. She walked around and stood in front of him, piercing intently in his eyes. "Are you saying you had no idea that Kyra had feelings for you?"

"I know she cares about me...I mean, I've been her patient for months now. That's to be expected."

"She cares about you in a romantic way, and I told her she needs to be careful because I don't want her to get hurt."

"Precious, there you go with the bullshit," Nico exhaled impatiently. "Why would you tell Kyra some shit like that. No wonder the vibe has been off with her recently," he shook his head.

"The vibe is off because Kyra's in love with you and doesn't know how to express it. It has nothing to do with what I said," Precious dismissed. "I just spoke out loud what everyone else has been saying to themselves. But you're an exceptionally smart man, Nico so I don't think any of this is surprising to you. Or maybe the real issue is that you have feelings for Kyra too?"

"Here you go." Nico grumbled.

"I could understand if you do. Like you said, she's been taking care of you for months now. It's natural for a bond to form. She's also a very pretty woman in a conservative, schoolteacher type way," Precious added.

"My focus isn't on a love connection right now. I'm tryna get out this wheelchair, so we can move on from you dissecting my relationship with Kyra. I want to hear about Aaliyah and Angel. How are my daughters doing?"

"They're doing great. I haven't spoken with Aaliyah in a couple days but the last time we did speak, she was in Miami with Angel. They've become super close, spending a great deal of time together. Just the way you always wanted," Precious smiled.

"That's the sort of news that motivates me to keep working hard and get the fuck out this wheelchair and back to my family."

"And you will, Nico. I see the progress you're making every single day. It makes me proud. I can't wait until I'm able to share this amazing news with everyone else."

"I wanna thank you again for respecting my decision," Nico conveyed to Precious. "You were intent on telling Aaliyah the truth but fortunately you changed your mind."

"You'll have to thank Supreme for that. He made an excellent argument as to why you being alive needed to remain a secret, at least for now," Precious conceded, sitting down on a bench near mature white pine trees that provided some much needed shade.

"I'll add that to an already extensive list of reasons I must thank Supreme. It's crazy but when he was looking for the place I'd stay at while I rehabilitated, I was completely against the house I'm living at now," Nico smiled widely.

"Why didn't you want to stay at that house? It's gorgeous and it's surrounded by so much beauty," Precious remarked admiring the color-ful floral display near the bog pond with stones leading to the two brooks that were decorated by the freshly bloomed Japanese primroses. Cross-ing the stone bridges, you could see where flame azaleas flourished in the center and on the edge of the meadow. There was also a fenced in gar-den containing a large collection of hostas. They ranged in sizes from miniature to giant and had various shades of blue, green, and yellow gold foliage, along with white and gold variegations. The splendid collection was a hidden jewel of serene beauty.

"Yeah, you right, it's gorgeous and the price reflected it. I thought it was a waste of fuckin' money. My mindset was on surviving surgery and living to see another day. All I wanted was someplace safe to stay while doing so. But Supreme, he said while I was worried about surviving, he was thinking about my recovery. He swore there was healing in nature and being surrounded by all this beauty that God created, would give me the strength I needed to fight to live."

"That sounds like Supreme," Precious laughed imagining her husband having that conversation with Nico.

"You know I thought he was crazy and on some Hollywood bullshit," Nico cracked. "But dammit that nigga was right," he chuckled. "Everything from the house, the outdoor area, living next to this nature trail and the gardens has played a pivotal role in my recovery. I feel crazy even saying this shit, but it's true. Environment matters when it comes to your overall mental health. I'm thankful Supreme wouldn't listen to me and did his shit his way."

"Does that mean I should stop being mad at him?" Precious considered her own question.

"I don't think you should've been mad at him in the first place. If anything, you should be mad at me. I'm the one that forced him into it by way of guilt. But that's something you and..."

"There you are. Sorry to interrupt," Kyra said walking over to Nico.

"No need to apologize, what's going on?"

"My mom just called, and she needs me to take her to her doctor's appointment tomorrow morning. My aunt was supposed to take her, but she cancelled at the last minute and because they're putting her under anesthesia, someone has to accompany her. I'm sorry for laying this on you at the last minute," Kyra explained.

"You don't ever have to tell me sorry for doing right by your mother," Nico insisted.

"I appreciate you being understanding. The appointment is early in the morning. If it's okay, I wanted to spend the night at my mom's house so I'm already there and won't be late. But Valerie is spending the night if you needed anything."

"Of course. Go be with your mother. I hope all goes well with her doctor's appointment."

"Thank you, Nico. I'll be back tomorrow

afternoon. Have a good evening."

"You too," he smiled.

"Should I be offended that Kyra didn't speak to me?" Precious gasped. "Or maybe she didn't see me sitting here. What do you think? Don't answer that question. I'm kidding of course. But I do hope everything is okay with her mother."

"So, do I," Nico said looking off in the distance.

"You seem concerned. I'm sure her mother will be fine."

"It's not that."

"Then what?" Precious pressed Nico for an answer.

"It's strange...out of nowhere I get hit with this unsettling energy. It's probably nothing. I think I'm just irritated due to hunger."

"Then we better go get you something to eat," Precious said getting up from the bench. "Do you know what you have the taste for?"

"Not sure but I'll figure it out by the time we get to the house," he said drifting back into his thoughts. Nico was unsure what sparked this sudden ominous mood, but he was unable to shake it which put him on guard.

Chapter Sixteen

About Last Night

Angel stood on the hotel balcony drinking a double expresso while taking in the stellar unobstructed panoramic views of the Miami skyline. She desperately needed the morning boost of caffeine from being up all night after Aaliyah's disastrous encounter with Gabriel. She continued to replay last night's tragic events, only garnering comfort from knowing the man responsible for her husband's murder was dead.

Angel was in the passenger seat of the dark tinted Escalade with Benito, one of her most trust-

ed goons. They had been parked outside the club for the last couple hours as she waited to hear from Aaliyah. Although she had three more men inside the club with eyes on Aaliyah, she was becoming shook-up that her sister hadn't made contact. So, when the call finally came through, Angel believed her distress would subside, but it was only heightened when she heard uncontrollable sobbing on the other end of the phone.

"Aaliyah, what's wrong, why are you crying... Aaliyah are you there?!" Angel shouted in the phone.

"I'm here..." Aaliyah's voice kept fading in and out which only made Angel more alarmed.

"Angel, it's me Amir," he said taking the phone from a discombobulated Aaliyah.

"Amir, what are you doing there?"

"It's a long story that I'll explain to you later, but right now we need your help."

"What can I do?" Angel was no longer leaning back in the passenger seat; she was sitting upright, and laser focused hanging onto Amir's every word.

"We have a dead man lying on the bathroom floor. Two of his bodyguards are posted right outside. I have business dealings with the club owner, so the dead body can be handled, but the two men out front with the guns are problematic."

"*Considered it handled. Let me make a call and I'll hit you right back.*"

"*Cool.*"

"*Amir, wait!*" *Angel yelled out before he hung up.*

"*Yeah.*"

"*Is Aaliyah okay...she's not hurt, is she?*" *Angel swallowed hard, scared to hear Amir's response.*

There was a long pause. "*She's upset but we'll get through this. I'm here and I got her,*" *Amir said putting Angel's mind at ease, which allowed her to concentrate on getting them out the club without incident.*

"*Two of Gabriel's bodyguards are posted in front of the bathroom. I need you all to get rid of them by any means necessary,*" *Angel expressed to Benito.* "*While you're getting rid of the bodyguards, have one of the men let off a couple shots in the club. Make sure they're careful not to hit anyone. I just need chaos to erupt so everyone will start fleeing. It's important the shots going off in the club and killing the bodyguards are timed to happen somewhat simultaneously. This will allow Amir and Aaliyah to get out the bathroom undetected, and for everyone in the club to be so caught up in escaping the gunfire that they barely pay attention to the two dead men.*"

"I like that plan," Benito nodded his head in agreement. "We can mos def pull that shit off."

"We short on time, so go get it done," Angel said sliding over to the driver's side, "I'll meet you across the street because this parking lot about to be chaotic," she told Benito before pulling off and placing a call to one of her henchmen in the club and then to Amir.

"What you got for me?" Amir questioned answering Aaliyah's phone.

"Someone is coming in now to handle the bodyguards. Get ready to bolt, because another one of my men is going to let out a few shots to cause pandemonium in the club. You know what to do when that happens."

"We on it."

"Amir, make sure you take care of my sister."

"Always," he vowed.

"Fuck, that didn't take long," Angel uttered looking out the rearview mirror. By the time she hung up with Amir, all hell had broken lose. Club-goers were fleeing in rapid speed as if the building was on fire. Angel's thoughts went back to Amir and Aaliyah. "Please don't let any harm come to them."

Angel reflecting on the events surrounding last night's nightmare came to an end when she heard a knock on the door.

"Good morning, did I come by too early?" Amir asked, looking like he hadn't slept all night.

"No, come on in. I'm wide awake but Aaliyah is still sleeping," Angel told him closing the door.

"I figured; she went through a lot last night." The anguish on Amir's face spoke volumes.

"By the time we got back to the hotel, Aaliyah wanted to take a shower and go to sleep. She hasn't had a chance to tell me what happened."

"That piece of shit tried to rape her," Amir revealed jaws clenching.

"What!" Angel stood up placing her hand over her mouth mortified and repulsed.

"It would've happened too if I hadn't been in that bathroom stall," Amir fumed, balling his fists furious at the thought Aaliyah came that close, to being violated.

"That animal is a murderer and a rapist." Angel felt her brain about to explode.

"How did Aaliyah end up with that demonic fuck anyway," Amir wondered out loud. "I don't even know the muthafuckas name."

"His name is Gabriel Cattaneo and he's responsible for the murder of my husband. I wanted retribution. It's my fault that Aaliyah became his next victim." Angel was consumed with guilt.

"None of this is your fault," Aaliyah said emerging from the bedroom.

"You're awake!" Angel hurried over to Aaliyah and held her tightly. "I'm so, so sorry I wasn't there to protect you. Thank God Amir was."

"Yes, thank God for Amir," Aaliyah looked over at him lovingly. "And this is not your fault, Angel. Gabriel started out being rough with me when I first sat down," she confessed shaking her head. "I should've never gone into that bathroom with him."

"But you wouldn't have been there in the first place if it wasn't for me."

"I volunteered...I wanted to do this. You didn't force me, Angel. I insisted it be me."

"Neither one of you are to blame," Amir spoke up and said. "That muthafucka was an animal and a junky. I guarantee this wasn't the first time he did something like this. He was way too comfortable."

"Amir is right," Aaliyah nodded.

"Hold on. This my father calling on my business phone," Amir said stepping off to the side to take the call. "Hey dad, what's going on?"

"I was checking on your whereabouts."

"I'm in Miami, why do you need me to come to New York?"

"No, that's exactly where I need you to be. I'm taking on a new business partner. His son is going to be the point person, and you're going to be my point person," Genesis laid out. "His son lives in Miami also."

"That works out perfect."

"Our sentiments exactly," Genesis agreed.

"So, when are we supposed to link up?" Amir wanted to know.

"Silvano should be in touch shortly with that information. When he does hit me back, I'll call you. I gave Silvano this number, so he might just pass it along to his son. His name is Gabriel Cattaneo, so look out for his call."

"Gabriel Cattaneo." Amir repeated the name out loud causing Aaliyah and Angel to pause amid their conversation and look over at him.

"Yes Gabriel. I'll call you when I hear back from Silvano, but just be prepared to meet with his son when he reaches out, which should be soon."

"I'll look out for his call," Amir said, knowing that was one call that would never be coming.

"What was that about? You already told your dad what happened last night?" Aaliyah asked, concerned it would get back to her parents before she had an opportunity to spin the story the way she wanted.

"No, I haven't told my dad anything."

"Then why did you mention Gabriel's name?" Angel was puzzled just like her sister.

Amir had to take a moment to digest what his father told him. He sat down on the couch and slumped his head back staring up at the ceiling.

"My dad has partnered up with some man named Silvano."

"Silvano!" Angel said the familiar name out loud, interrupting Amir. "That's Gabriel's father."

"Exactly. Silvano's son is supposed to be contacting me because we're going to be doing business together," Amir sighed deeply.

"Fuck!" Aaliyah flopped down on the couch next to Amir. "Your dad would be doing business with a major mafia crime boss."

"How am I gonna tell my dad that Gabriel Cattaneo is dead and I'm the one who killed him," Amir contemplated.

Chapter Seventeen

It Was Written

Shiffon had been feeling fatigued for the last couple weeks. She didn't think much of it because besides the constant drama she was involved in, she also remained on the move nonstop. Feeling tired came with the territory. But then nausea started kicking in, followed with vomiting, frequent urination and breast tenderness. Shiffon always had an irregular menstrual cycle, so at this point, she decided taking a home pregnancy test would be the only way to confirm if she was with child. After three positive tests, she was confident she was carrying Maverick's baby. But before sharing the news, Shiffon made an appointment with an OBGYN to determine how far along she was. So, while she was consumed with her pregnancy, unbeknownst to Shiffon she was being tracked by a deranged woman.

Mia turned into a complete stalker. She had been putting in work in an attempt to track Shiffon's every move. She found the woman at the center of her obsession didn't do much. She barely left the hotel she was staying at in Rittenhouse Square but that didn't stop Mia's fixation. She convinced herself that Shiffon was having a full fledge torrid affair with Caleb. So, when Mia followed Shiffon to an Obstetrics & Gynecology office on Chestnut Street, she lost her freakin' mind.

"That bitch is pregnant with Caleb's baby!" Mia sat in her car bawling, punching the steering wheel repeatedly. She broke out in a cold sweat with a rapid irregular heartbeat and pulse, as her heart continued to race, pounding out of her chest. She felt like she wasn't getting enough oxygen, just as you would at high attitude. She became light-headed and dizzy. Mia was experiencing all the symptoms of a heart attack but of course it was a self-induced panic attack. "You will never have Caleb's baby! Never!" She wailed like a woman completely unhinged.

Mia wiped away her tears and became possessed with resoluteness. She refused to crumble. This tormenting pain became Mia's motivation. It was time to execute her plan of attack. The death clock had begun ticking for Shiffon.

A premonition that doom was looming had Nico experiencing a sleepless night. The tossing, turning and uncertainty made him feel isolated. What triggered this cloud of darkness to hover over him remained a mystery. What made matters worse was when he would doze off Nico became engrossed in a haunting dream. He was gripping his wheelchair moving forward through the nature trail. The sky was translucent, and he was surrounded by exquisite and colorful floral arrangements. The glorious scenery was surreal. Nico absorbed the remarkable beauty continuing through the trails but the further he went the crystal-clear skies began to darken until it was monopolized in murkiness. The flawless and vibrant flowers were now unsightly and vapid.

Nico kept pushing forward faster and faster

to escape what had turned into a place of misery that only a moment ago was an ethereal oasis. He was maneuvering the trails at a high speed to make his exit, but the wheelchair smashed against a stone bordering the pond breaking his stride. When he caught a glimpse of his reflection in the water, he noticed a dead body turned face down. Nico turned the body over and was startled when it was Kyra's face staring back at him.

"What the fuck is going on!" Nico was breathing heavy with sweat dowsing his forehead when he woke up from his dream that seemed more like a nightmare. He looked over at the digital clock and it was 2:15 in the morning. "Damn, I gotta piss," he said lifting himself out the bed to get in his wheelchair. Nico was halfway to the bathroom when he heard what sounded like the front door opening. His senses were acute, and that familiar ominous aura confirmed what Nico already knew—his life was in grave danger.

Nico took hold of the hand rims that was near the rear wheels and propelled his wheelchair forward to the nightstand, where two guns Supreme had gotten for him were located. Nico hadn't fired a weapon in what seemed like an eternity, but he knew it was kill or be killed. In an attempt to alert security to the danger upon him and everyone else in the house, he reached over to press the alarm button but there was no time. The locked bedroom door was kicked in and mayhem proceeded.

"We seem to keep ending up here at the same time," Dominique said to Justina with a sugary smile. "But we both share a child with Desmond, so it should be expected."

"I suppose but I highly doubt our run-ins are by accident. My guess is that you knew I would be here to pick up Desi and slithered your pathetic ass over here to sniff behind Desmond," Justina summarized.

"I thought we were past these petty jabs," Dominique chided.

"Not sure where that idea came from," Justina raised an eyebrow. "Certainly not because you pushed out a baby and now you're a mother," she mocked.

"Desi is a big brother to Chloe. They're brother and sister. That alone should make us try to be cordial to one another."

"Where is Desmond? I wanted to see him before I got Desi and left."

"I'm sure you do but Desmond is in his office on a business call. He might be awhile. But when he comes out, I'll let him know you stopped by," Dominique winked.

"Are you staying here with Desmond?" Justina felt her blood pressure rising.

"If I was, why would you care? You're married to another man."

"Bitch, don't fuck with me!" Justina spit, walking up on Dominique.

"I think you need to calm down." Dominique raised her finger pointing it towards Justina's face, which she quickly slapped away.

"I will break that bony finger if you put it in my face again," Justina threatened.

"Your jealously is really getting the best of you Justina," Dominique taunted her nemesis. "But you must learn to let it go. I'm the mother of Desmond's *biological* child." She stressed the word biological in an attempt to get Justina to snap. "I'm not going anywhere."

Justina wanted to put her foot up Dominique's ass. But she knew that would be giving her what she craved, an excuse to run to Desmond playing the victim.

"I know you think because I divorced Desmond that left the door wide open for you. But you'll never be able to fill my shoes and a baby won't get you the ring."

"Maybe you're right or maybe you're wrong. A baby might not get me the ring, but it will get me back in his bed," Dominique boasted.

"You really are a desperate, pathetic slut!"

"So, you say. But I consider myself a resource-ful woman who is trying to do what is best for her child. Chloe deserves to have a close relation-ship with her father. A sensible way to guarantee that is by making sure my bond with Desmond remains intact. What better way is there for two people to stay connected than through intima-cy. Desmond is a man with needs. And we both know what an insatiable sexual appetite he has," Dominique prodded, further provoking Justina.

"I'm sure Desi is ready. I can speak with Desmond later."

Justina grabbed her belongings and stormed off to get her son. Dominique watched with amusement. Her ultimate goal was to annoy Justina to the point, that she would stop com-ing around and send her nanny to retrieve Desi instead. Dominique couldn't afford to have her anywhere around until she cemented herself in Desmond's life. She knew Desmond was still in love with his ex-wife but after her conversation with Justina, it confirmed that so was she.

As Justina was securing Desi in his car seat, she debated a minimum of four times on whether to go back inside Desmond's house and wait for him to finish his business call. She didn't have a reason to see her ex-husband other than Justina missed him. Instead of staying she made the decision to leave, even though that meant giving Dominique the win.

"I gave that bitch the win the moment I divorced my husband," Justina mumbled slamming her car door shut. She turned back and stared at Desi who was already falling asleep. He was her everything and so was her marriage at one time. As her anger diminished, Justina regretted divorcing Desmond over his indiscretion with Dominique. She should've fought for her marriage and because she didn't, Dominique was determined to be the only woman in Desmond's life. This left Justina torn because although she was in love with her ex, she did love Amir too. It wasn't the type of love she shared with Desmond where even when they weren't touching—their breath and heart rates naturally fell into sync with each other. When Justina and Desmond cuddled, their chest would be rising and falling as one. That's how deep their love ran.

Justina's love for Amir remained strong but more so because its foundation was built from a safe place. But her passion and heart belonged to Desmond. Their emotional ties would likely last a lifetime, but Justina remained committed to Amir. She wanted their marriage to work, if for no other reason than for the beautiful son they shared together.

Chapter Eighteen

Nine Lives

In what had become her new daily routine, Precious arrived that morning at Nico's place, looking forward to watching him exercise in the pool with his physical therapist, while she devoured her favorite muffins. She knocked on the door and rang the doorbell but there was no response.

"Maybe everyone is outside in the back," Precious speculated out loud, ringing the doorbell one more time before deciding to turn the knob. It was open and all seemed well when she first entered the foyer. But then she came upon the first dead body once entering the kitchen to get a cup of coffee that Valerie made each morning. The older woman's stiffened body was slumped over the kitchen island with a bullet in her head. She was wearing her pajamas and bathrobe. The pool of blood appearing to be crimson, and purple settled around her head, creating a blotchy pattern.

Before Precious could catch her breath, she ran towards Nico's room fearing what awaited her. When she turned down the hallway there was another dead body right outside the bedroom door. He was dressed in all black with shots to the chest. Precious stepped over his corpse and entered Nico's bedroom, first noticing his wheelchair in the far corner. There was another dead body near the bathroom entrance, and she began to break down in tears believing it was Nico. But as she got closer it was another man dressed in all black dead with two gunshots to the head.

Where the fuck is Nico! All these dead bodies and no Nico, Precious thought to herself fighting back tears. She wasn't sure what to do so she called Supreme.

"Hey baby, what's up?" Supreme answered evenly unaware of the dire news that awaited him on the other end of the phone.

"Supreme, you need to get here now." Her voice was trembling.

"Precious, what's wrong?"

"There're three dead bodies in this house and could be more. And I can't find Nico!" Precious sounded hysterical. "I see his wheelchair but not him. Do you think he was kidnapped?"

"Where are you in the house?" Supreme questioned.

"In Nico's bedroom."

"Okay, I want you to do something for me. Go inside the bedroom closet. You'll see three custom built-in cabinets. Underneath each cabinet is a light. Behind the middle cabinet light is a small button. Do you feel it?"

"Yes, I feel it."

"Good, press that button and a door on the other side of the closet is going to open. Call out Nico's name so he knows it's you."

"Nico! Nico, are you in there?" Precious called out. She could hear some movement and then a few moments later Nico emerged walking, barely but he was walking with a gun in each hand. "Dear God! Nico!"

"Are you gonna help an old man out," Nico cracked, doing his best to stay upright. Precious hurried over to be his crutch.

"Babe, you tend to Nico. Stay in the bedroom and lock the door until I get there with some backup," Supreme said ending the call.

"You have to stop scaring me. I thought I lost you again," Precious confessed helping Nico over to the bed.

"Shit, I scared my damn self when my ass had enough fuckin' courage to walk," he chuckled.

"Glad you can find humor in this bullshit because I'm gettin' too old for all this mayhem," Precious said walking over to the dead body in the hallway to retrieve the gun before closing the bedroom door and locking it. She figured they were no longer in imminent danger but Precious wanted to take precautions.

"I been too old for this shit, but it is what it is," Nico moaned, observing the dead body near the bathroom entrance. "That muthafucka right there is the reason I'm back walking. I guess I should thank that dead nigga for tryna kill me."

"I'm having a hard time wrapping my head around what happened. I come in the house, and I see Valerie dead in the kitchen..."

"Fuck! He shouted, cutting Precious off. They got Valerie." That news weighed heavy on Nico's heart. "Was any other staff here?"

"Honestly, I'm not sure. After I saw Valerie's

body, I ran in here to check on you. What about your physical therapist did he come this morning?"

"No, he called last night saying he needed to cancel."

"What about Kyra...oh that's right," Precious caught herself. "She had to take her mother to the doctor. Who else might be here?"

"At least one security guard stays the night. I think last night Calvin was on duty. There is also a woman named Beatrice that is normally here. I'm not sure if you've ever met her. The other staff members typically rotate."

"Obviously, this hit was meant for you, but how do you think they found your location?" she asked.

"I wish I knew, but you know what's crazy."

"What?" Precious sat down next to Nico on the bed.

"For the last couple days, I had this eerie fuckin' feeling but I thought maybe my mind was playin' tricks on me. But last night I couldn't really sleep and woke up. That's when I heard someone coming into the house. It was like I knew they were coming. I had already mentally prepared myself."

"Is that why you seemed to be preoccupied

yesterday when we were at the botanical garden?"

"Yes," Nico sighed deeply. "I hoped it wouldn't happen, but we always knew there was a possibility they would find my location. Hence the reason Supreme gave me these guns and installed a hidden safe room in the closet. He keeps, keeping me alive," Nico chuckled. "Fuck, at this rate, I'ma forever be indebted to that nigga," he shrugged.

"You're alive, which is all I care about," Precious said leaning her head on Nico's shoulder.

Nico was grateful to be alive also. He came up through the streets of hard knocks and graduated at the top of his class too. For that reason, when he was younger, he compared himself to the myth of a cat having nine lives, which was related to the fact that falling cats can twist in midair and land on their feet. It led many to assume that cats have multiple lives because they can handle falling from great heights and the belief that they can see in total darkness. Like a wild cat, Nico's survival skills had served him well also, but after his latest brush with death, he believed his multiple swings at life was coming to an end, and his nine lives were running out.

Chapter Nineteen

Broken Promises

"I was beginning to think you had done another disappearing act on me," Genesis remarked when he answered Supreme's call.

"Listen, I need you to meet me at my house in about an hour," Supreme said ignoring Genesis' comment.

"Can we make it two? I'm on my way to meet with Silvano."

"That works, but come over right after you're done meeting with Silvano," Supreme insisted.

"Is everything okay?"

"No, everything is not okay. Maverick is very much alive."

"Wait...what? Turn that music down," Genesis ordered his driver from the back wanting to make sure he heard Supreme correctly.

"Maverick is alive. When you see Silvano, make sure you mention that shit to him."

"How do you know?" Genesis was not fully convinced.

"I'll explain in detail when you come over, but he sent his hitters."

"Fuck!" Genesis punched his fist into the imperial blue leather seat. "I thought that nigga was dead and he still lurking in the dark." His anger was smoldering.

"That's why I wanted to put you on notice. We'll further discuss when I see you."

"Cool." Genesis hung up with Supreme and placed calls to Amir and Caleb. They needed to be warned and take steps to protect themselves. With Maverick on the loose there was no telling what he might pull, but they were all in danger.

"Babe, did you decide where you wanted to go for lunch?" Mia asked when she got out the shower, brushing her hand across Caleb's bare chest.

"Not right now," he said pushing Mia's hand away. "Hold on, I need to make a call." Caleb got out of bed and went into the living room.

"I'll get dressed that way I'll be ready whenever you decide," Mia said standing outside the door so she could ear hustle.

"Hey Caleb."

"Shiffon, do you have a moment to talk?" Caleb's voice had a sense of urgency which meant there was no time for a proper greeting.

"Sure, what's up?"

"I just got a call from Genesis. Maverick is still alive. This nigga just won't die."

Shiffon pulled over in her car. This was the call she'd been dreading, but never did she predict it would come this soon.

"But I was under the impression it had been confirmed Maverick was dead."

"So did I, but supposedly he sent his hitters to take out some of Genesis' people."

"Who did he target?" Shiffon asked although she was pretty sure she knew the answer.

"I don't know all the details yet. Genesis wanted to warn me, make sure I stay strapped. You stay strapped too. I'm sure you're on his hit list since he knows you were hired to kill him."

"Thank you for keeping me in the loop. I will for sure stay strapped and watch my back. Keep me posted if you get any updates," Shiffon told Caleb.

"I will. Are you in the A?"

"No, I'm still in Philly. That new job I accepted kept me in town."

"Cool. Before you leave, if you get some free time I wanna link up for dinner, drinks or both," Caleb made known.

"I'd like that. I'll hit you up when I have some down time," she told Caleb, anxious to get off the phone. Her mind was on Maverick. He'd been out of town and was due to return today. She needed answers and wanted to confront him asap. "Talk to you soon," Shiffon said to Caleb.

"Yep, talk to you soon."

Mia hurried over to the bed and pretended to be watching television when she heard Caleb end his call with Shiffon.

"Have you decided what you wanna do?" Mia kept her tone very detached.

"I'ma take a shower, then we can get ready to," Caleb said placing his phone on the dresser before going into the bathroom.

"Sounds good. I'll get dressed." Mia waited a couple minutes until she knew Caleb was safely in the shower and then grabbed his phone. It took her weeks of dedicated nosiness to break his passcode. She could never catch the last two digits, but once she got the first four and realized they were the month and day of Amelia's birthday, she added the year and boom it hit.

Mia had been patiently waiting for when she could use the information to her advantage, and it had finally presented itself. Mia sent Shiffon a text.

Just spoke to Genesis again. Got update about Maverick. Need to discuss in person. Can you meet me at 6?

Mia got excited when she saw the three little dots hover in a conversation bubble indicating Shiffon was replying.

Sure I can meet @ 6. Let me know where.

After Mia sent Shiffon the address, she deleted the messages so there would be no trace on Caleb's phone. *Good riddance Shiffon,* Mia smiled ready to delete her for good.

"Maverick, I was hoping you would be here," Shiffon smiled, closing the hotel room door. "I missed you," she said falling into his arms.

"I missed you too, baby," he said giving her a kiss.

Before she spoke with Caleb, this was supposed to be the moment she told Maverick the baby news. Shiffon envisioned his reaction and them both wondering if she was carrying a boy or a girl. But that conversation would have to wait.

"Caleb called me when I was on my way back to the hotel."

"Really...what did he want?"

"He wanted me to know you were still alive." Shiffon paid close attention to Maverick's facial expression. He kept it blank.

"Is that right? Did he tell you how he came to that conclusion?"

"Genesis told him. Supposedly you sent your hitters to take out his people. Please tell me this has nothing to do with Nico?"

"What did Caleb say?" Maverick was being restrained with his answers.

"I want you to tell me?"

"No, you don't. We already discussed this re-member." Maverick stretched his body out on the chair and turned on the television. He was purposedly giving disinterested vibes.

"I asked you not to make a move on Nico. That it was too risky. Now look what you've done. You've ignited a war that had ended."

"Ended for who because it damn sure hadn't ended for me. And it won't until Genesis and his entire crew are dead."

"Is this the life you want for yourself...for us?"

"Shiffon, you know who I am and what I do. The same goes for you. We're not like everyone else...we move differently."

"At some point things change, Maverick. I don't want to be a hired killer for the rest of my life. And I would hope you feel the same way."

"This is who I am, Shiffon. Was it my intent to go to war with Genesis...no. But he started it and I have no choice but to finish it," Maverick reasoned.

"You do have a choice; we all have a choice and I choose our baby."

"Baby...did you say baby?" Maverick cut off the television and turned to Shiffon. "You're pregnant?"

"Yes. Almost eight weeks."

"How long have you known?"

"I just found out a few days ago."

"You're carrying my baby!" Maverick came over placing his hand on Shiffon's midriff. "My baby is having my baby," he grinned widely. "That's a beautiful thing."

Maverick's loving reaction warmed Shiffon's hear. "It is a beautiful thing. That's why we have to cut ties here and start our life over somewhere else," she urged.

"I can't do that right now. I'm not saying I won't do it at some point, but not right now."

"What about our baby? Do you not care that I can end up dead behind this vendetta you have with Genesis?"

"You mean the vendetta Genesis has against me," Maverick shot back indignantly.

"I can't do this with you right now. It's not just about us anymore, Maverick. There's a baby growing inside me that I want to live to see."

"And you will."

"So you say. But a bullet knows no name." Shiffon stated cautiously. "I have somewhere I need to be," she eyed her watch. "Think about what I said. We can finish our conversation when

I get back." Shiffon blew Maverick a kiss and her last three words before leaving were I love you.

Chapter Twenty

Almost There

Silvano was sitting behind an elongated antique wood desk accentuated by a contemporary white office chair with a matching long white sofa that was directly across from the fireplace. The spacious wood-paneled luxury home office had a dome ceiling, extensive custom built-in shelving and cabinetry, with double doors leading to the patio. It was a perfect blend of luxurious Mediterranean style mixed with an old-world design. With all the trappings of success and wealth, most would miss the telltale signs of the misery looming in the air.

When Genesis walked into Silvano's office, he got up from his chair and stood in front of a huge window overlooking the ocean. He was visibly in deep thought, and Genesis noticed Silvano also didn't have his signature cigar in his mouth.

"Please have a seat." Genesis sat down on the long white sofa, but Silvano had yet to turn around.

"Is everything alright with you, Silvano? You don't seem like yourself."

"This has been a difficult last few days for me."

"I figured such when you never got back in touch with me to set up a time and day for my son and your son to meet. Have the difficulties been smoothed out?" Genesis asked shifting his position on the sofa.

"Unfortunately, it has not. My son is missing."

"Gabriel?"

"Yes," Silvano confirmed.

"I'm sorry to hear that."

"Me too. I believe my son is dead," he said matter-of-factly.

"Damn, Silvano. Why do you think Gabriel is dead?"

"The last place anyone saw him was at a

nightclub in Miami. The security detail that was with him that night, both men are dead. No one has spoken to my son since that night including me."

"That doesn't sound promising," Genesis acknowledged. "I wonder if the situation with Gabriel has anything to do with what I need to discuss with you."

"What do you need to discuss with me?"

"Maverick isn't dead."

"Maverick? Why does that name sound familiar?" Silvano asked.

"After you located Maverick in Fiji, you sent your men to kill him on my behalf."

"Yes, yes, now I remember. You're saying that man isn't dead?"

"He's very much alive. I got word on my way over here to see you that Maverick came at my people again."

"How did this happen," Silvano shook his head. "My men brought me back proof. Genesis, I have once again not honored our agreement. I will make this right," he vowed.

"You said your men brought you proof. What sort of proof?"

"A few items they confiscated from the bungalow after they killed them, or whoever they killed," Silvano said flustered over his men fuck-ing up. "I planned on giving the items to you but there useless now."

"If you don't mind, I would appreciate if you could hand me over those items," Genesis re-quested.

"Of course. It's the least I can do," Silvano said pulling open the bottom drawer on his desk and retrieving a small bag containing the items and handed it to Genesis.

"Thank you."

"You mentioned my son's disappearance having something to do with this botched hit. Do you think this Maverick man is responsible for my son going missing?"

"I can't say for sure. But Maverick is extreme-ly resourceful. If he somehow found out that it was your men that tried to kill him, he would want to retaliate."

"I see. If he did have something to do with my son's disappearance, then your enemy has now also become my enemy."

"Maybe if we put our minds together, we can rid this Maverick problem permanently. Because he has proven to be a formidable enemy."

"We can shake on that, Genesis." Silvano ex-tended his hand. "I give you, my word. My men will continue to hunt Maverick down until he is no longer a problem for you or for me."

"Thank you. Let me know if there's anything I can do to help locate your son. We can table doing that other business together until we find out what happened to Gabriel."

"No need to wait. I want to move forward with our new business venture. I have someone I am considering replacing Gabriel with, if it comes to that."

"That decision is yours to make. Amir is prepared to move forward whenever you are," Genesis made clear.

"I've always appreciated your patience, Genesis. And unlike me, you've continuously shown you're a man of your word. But I vow to show you the same. I will be in touch within the next few days." Salvino walked Genesis to the door, wanting to assure him that even with the recent setbacks, their business relationship would prove to be conducive for them both.

When Genesis left Silvano's estate and got back in the car, he took a moment to peruse the items retrieved from the bungalow Maverick was staying at in Fiji. It wasn't until he came across one particular item was his interest elevated. He immediately placed a call to Caleb.

"Boss, what can I do for you?"

"Caleb, I need you in NYC asap. When can you get here?"

"I can leave Philly and be on the way within the hour," Caleb said, with no intention of keeping his boss waiting.

"Good. Call me the moment you arrive," Genesis said hanging up with Caleb. He then sent Supreme a text letting him know he was on the way.

5 minutes away, was the text Shiffon sent to Caleb in route to where they were meeting.

During the entire drive, Shiffon was on the verge of tears. She wasn't typically the overly emotional type, so she was blaming it on pregnancy hormones, but Maverick had her heart hurting. His obsession with taking down Genesis was destroying any chance they had of starting their lives over together somewhere else. If she wasn't pregnant Shiffon would be more inclined to go on this journey with Maverick but the baby she was carrying changed everything. A healthy pregnancy was her top priority. She was praying that soon Maverick would view things the same way—being alive to raise their child superseded his feud with Genesis. In the meantime, Shiffon was struggling with what she desired to do and what she felt forced into.

Now I have to meet with Caleb and pretend I don't know what the fuck is really going on. I hate doing this shit. Pretending to be loyal to my assignment as an assassin but in bed with the man I was hired to kill. She was ready for the charade to come to an end, Shiffon thought to herself pulling into the driveway at the house she was meeting Caleb.

Knock...knock...knock

"That's Caleb calling me now," Shiffon said out loud about to answer the phone until the front door opened.

"Hi, Shiffon!" Mia smiled cheerfully.

"Hey...who are you?"

"I'm Mia, a friend of Caleb."

"He just called me," Shiffon said reaching for her phone to call him back.

"Yeah, he was probably calling to let you know he's running a few minutes late, but he told me to let you come in and have a seat while you wait," Mia said sweetly.

"Sure," Shiffon agreed thinking that the woman appeared harmless. Mia closed the door disguising her sinister plan with a gracious smile.

"Can I get you anything?" Mia offered.

"You know what, it's so hot outside, can I get some water, with ice."

"Of course. I'll be right back," Mia said going into the kitchen.

Shiffon checked her phone and saw that Caleb sent her a text to call him.

"Hey, Caleb. Where you at?" Shiffon asked.

"On my way to NYC. Where you?"

"NYC?! I'm here waiting..." Those were the last words Shiffon spoke before she dropped her phone and her body slumped to the hardwood floor.

"All you had to do was stay away from my man," Mia hissed swinging the 16-pound Kidde Proline 10MP fire extinguisher to the back of Shiffon's head, knocking her out cold. She walked around to get Shiffon's phone and could hear Caleb yelling out her name. Mia started stumping on the iPhone and then slammed the fire extinguisher down, shattering it in half. She had plans for Shiffon and Mia didn't want any interruptions.

Chapter Twenty-One

Dead Or Alive

When the driver pulled through the Tuscan wrought iron double gates to the private, palatial estate there were several SUVs lined up the circular driveway in front of the stone chateau.

"Caleb is supposed to be here in about thirty minutes. When he arrives come get me," Genesis told his driver before heading inside to meet with Supreme.

Genesis was greeted by Precious after ringing the doorbell. "Thank you for coming." She wrapped her arms around Genesis and held him closely.

"Of course, I would come. Why would you think otherwise?" he asked trying to get a read on Precious while they stood in the foyer.

"Maybe I expressed that wrong. Thank you for coming because I need you to be here."

"You wanna tell me what's going on, because when I spoke to Supreme earlier, he sounded agitated. I pull up and there's a fleet of SUVs in the driveway and now looking at you, I'm concerned about your overall wellbeing. What's really happening around here, Precious?"

"I think there's someone who can explain what seemed like the unexplainable to you better than I can." Genesis followed behind Precious who led him through the elegant 11,000 sq. ft. mansion that had white marble, stone tile and oak hardwood floors throughout. When they entered the dramatic two-story great room, Genesis's eyes instantly zoomed in on a tall, lean man who was standing next to the fireplace with his back towards them, holding a cane in his right hand.

"I'll leave the two of you alone to talk," Precious said going upstairs to the theater room where Supreme and the security detail were.

The room was hauntingly silent. Genesis didn't understand why Precious left him alone to talk with a man who at this point was a stranger to him. This seemed like some bizarre shit, but he also knew there had to be a logical explanation.

"I'm not sure what's going on but um can you turn around so I can see who I'm speaking to," Genesis said walking closer to the man.

"Only if you promise to stay cool," Nico turned around and said to a shook Genesis, who couldn't even speak for several seconds. He gawked in disturbed amazement believing his eyes were playing a cruel trick on him.

"What tha fuck...is this shit even real?" Genesis was shaking his head in disbelief.

"It's real, Genesis. I'm alive."

"My brother." Tears escaped Genesis' eyes as he locked his arms around Nico and the two men embraced. "Man, you got so much fuckin' explaining to do." Both men laughed.

"You right I do, but first let's discuss what's happening right now," Nico said as they walked over to the sofa and sat down. "Maverick sent his hitters to kill me. I was able to take out two of his men, but they killed three of mine. Not sure how he tracked my location, as we're still investigating that shit. But for now, I'll be staying here with

Supreme and Precious."

"I'm sick of hearing that nigga's name," Genesis scoffed. "Do you think it was an inside job."

"Not sure. Initially I said no but at this point anything is possible. You know how the game go when you at war," Nico said nodding his head, signaling someone else had come into the room.

"Caleb is here," Genesis' driver informed him.

"I'll be right out," he told his driver before turning his attention back to Nico. "Let me go out and speak to Caleb for a minute. It'll only take a minute."

"Take your time. I'm not going anywhere," Nico smiled.

"Man, I don't believe none of that shit. I might need you to move in wit' me instead, so I can keep both my eyes on you," Genesis joked.

When Genesis got outside, he opened the back door to get one of the items he received from Silvano. Caleb was sitting in his Range Rover and appeared to be on a phone call, so he waited until he was done.

"Sorry about that boss," Caleb said, hopping out the truck.

"Don't worry about it. I appreciate you getting here quickly.

"No doubt. I could tell it was important."

"It is. I want you to take a look at something," Genesis said giving Caleb a necklace with a heart locket on it.

"Whose necklace is this?" he asked inspecting the delicate gold heart.

"Open the locket," Genesis directed. "Who is that a picture of."

"Shiffon, and her little brother," Caleb confirmed.

"That's what I thought."

"Where did you get this?" Caleb questioned.

"Silvano. His men confiscated it from the bungalow in Fiji where Maverick was staying," Genesis informed his protégé. "You know what that means."

"Hold up." Caleb took a step back, soaking in the implications Genesis was making. "Are you saying Shiffon is involved with Maverick on some romantic type of shit?"

"I doubt she was all the way in Fiji on a church retreat and her necklace just so happened to end up in Maverick's bungalow."

"Maybe she was working, you know got hired for an assassin assignment and..." Caleb's voice faded off trying to think of a justifiable reason Shiffon's necklace would end up at the same place Maverick had been staying.

"And what? Have you seen her in the last few weeks?"

"Yeah, I've seen her."

"At any time did Shiffon mention seeing or being in contact with Maverick or going to Fiji?"

"No, she didn't."

"You go find Shiffon and bring her to me," Genesis commanded pointing his finger in Caleb's face.

"I'll get right on it."

"You do that, Caleb. Bring that woman to me. I need to find out everything she knows about Maverick. Because if she's fuckin' that nigga, it would explain a lot of this bullshit."

"It would but Genesis, I know this chick. She would never be on no foul bullshit like that."

"I'll make that determination. Just bring her to me asap."

Aaliyah, Angel and Amir were sipping white wine waiting for their chartered private jet to take off from Opa-Locka Executive Airport in Miami, Florida. They were making small talk, doing everything possible to avoid speaking about the murder of Gabriel Cattaneo and the pivotal role each of them played.

"Did your dad give you any indication why it was so urgent you come to New York?" Aaliyah asked Amir, scrolling through some pics on her phone.

"Nope. What about Precious?"

"My mom was extra vague too. She pretty much ordered me to get on a flight to New York and bring Angel," Aaliyah shrugged.

"That's the part that threw me off. Your mother's insistence that I come too. I'm not complaining about the invite, just curious to know why," Angel said holding up her glass as the flight attendant poured her some more wine.

"The flight is about to take off, so I say let's sit back and relax because we will know the answer to our question shortly," Amir announced fastening his seatbelt.

"Is it just me or are you all feeling a bit drowsy?" Aaliyah wanted to know.

"I am too, but I figured it's because this is my third glass of wine and I'm a bit tipsy," Angel yawned. "It don't take much for me to get a buzz."

"I haven't slept in like two fuckin' days so shit I need a nap," Amir sighed softly, closing his eyes.

Amir, Angel and Aaliyah eventually all dozed off for a few hours. Angel woke up first, but she was sluggish and in a daze. She was about to close her eyes and go back to sleep until she realized both her wrists were handcuffed to her seat.

"What the fuck!" Angel tried to shout but her voice was practically inaudible. Amir and Aaliyah begun to come out their daze soon after.

"We're still not in New York?" Aaliyah mumbled. "Is this a joke? Why am I handcuffed to my seat?" she barked shaking her arms trying to get the cuffs off.

"Yo, this shit ain't no joke. We been hijacked." Amir hated to say the shit out loud.

A man came from behind the cockpit carrying heavy artillery. He hovered over the three of them with a menacing demeanor.

"There's been a slight change with your flight reservation. We making a detour courtesy of Maverick McClay. We should be reaching our destination in the next hour. I advise ya to do what tha fuck I say and maybe you won't die."

Amir, Aaliyah and Angel glanced at each other and none of them had to say a word, their facial expressions spoke it all. Their lives were now in the hands of a diabolical killer.

Coming Soon

A KING PRODUCTION

The Legacy

Keep The Family Close...

A Novel

JOY DEJA KING

Chapter One

Raised By Wolves

"Alejo, we've been doing business for many years and my intention is for there to be many more. But I do have some concerns..."

"That's why we're meeting today," Alejo interjected, cutting Allen off. I've made you a very wealthy man. You've made millions and millions of dollars from my family..."

"And you've made that and much more from

our family," Clayton snapped, this time being the one to cut Alejo off. "So let's acknowledge this being a mutual beneficial relationship between both of our families."

Alejo slit his eyes at Clayton, feeling disrespected, his anger rested upon him. Clayton was the youngest son of Allen Collins but also the most vocal. Alejo then turned towards his son Damacio who sat calmly not saying a word in his father's defense, which further enraged the dictator of the Hernandez family.

An ominous quietness engulfed the room as the Collins family remained seated on one side of the table and the Hernandez family occupied the other.

"I think we can agree that over the years we've created a successful business relationship that works for all parties involved," Kasir said, speaking up and trying to be the voice of reason and peacemaker for what was quickly turning into enemy territory. "No one wants to create new problems. We only want to fix the one we currently have so we can all move forward."

"Kasir, I've always liked you," Alejo said with a half smile. "You've continuously conducted yourself with class and respect. Others can learn a lot from you."

"Others, meaning your crooked ass nephews," Clayton barked not ignoring the jab Alejo was taking at him. He then pointed his finger at Felipe and Hector, making sure that everyone at the table knew exactly who he was speaking of since there were a dozen family members on the Hernandez side of the table.

Chaos quickly erupted within the Hernandez family as the members began having a heated exchange amongst each other. They were speaking Spanish and although neither Allen nor Clayton understood what was being said, Kasir spoke the language fluently.

"Dad, I think we need to fall back and not let this meeting get any further out of control. Let's table this discussion for a later date," Kasir told his father in a very low tone.

"Fuck that! We ain't tabling shit. As much money as we bring to this fuckin' table and these snakes want to short us. Nah, I ain't having it. That shit ends today," Clayton stated, not backing down.

"You come here and insult me and my family with your outrageous accusations," Alejo stood up and yelled, pushing back the single silver curl that kept falling over his forehead. "I will not tolerate such insults from the likes of you. My family does good business. You clearly cannot say the same."

"This is what you call good business," Clayton shot back, placing his iPhone on the center of the table. Then pressing play on the video that was sent to him.

Alejo grabbed the phone from off the table and watched the video intently, scrutinizing every detail. After he was satisfied he then handed it to his son Damacio, who after viewing, passed it around to the other family members at the table.

"What's on that video?" Kasir questioned his brother.

"I want to know the same thing," his father stated.

"Let's just say that not only are those two motherfuckers stealing from us, they're stealing from they own fuckin' family too," Clayton huffed, leaning back in his chair, pleased that he had the proof to back up his claims.

"We owe your family an apology," Damacio said, as his father sat back down in his chair with a glaze of defeat in his eyes. It was obvious the old man hated to be wrong and had no intentions of admitting it, so his son had to do it for him.

"Does that mean my concerns will be addressed and handled properly?" Allen Collins questioned.

"Of course. You have my word that this matter will be corrected in the very near future and there is no need for you to worry, as it won't happen again. Please accept my apology on behalf of my entire family," Damacio said, reaching over to shake each of their hands.

"Thank you, Damacio," Allen said giving a firm handshake. "I'll be in touch soon."

"Of course. Business will resume as usual and we look forward to it," Damacio made clear before the men gathered their belongings and began to make their exit.

"Wait!" shouted Alejo. The Collins men stopped in their tracks and turned towards him.

"Father, what are you doing?" Damacio asked, confused by his sudden outburst.

"There is something that needs to be addressed and no one is leaving this room until it's done," Alejo demanded.

With smooth ease, Clayton rested his arm towards the back of his pants, placing his hand on the Glock 20–10mm auto. Before the meeting, the Collins' men had agreed to have their security team wait outside in the parking lot instead of coming in the building, so it wouldn't be a hostile environment. But that didn't stop Clayton from taking his own precautions. He eyed his brother Kasir who maintained his typical calm demeanor that annoyed the fuck out of Clayton.

"Alejo, what else needs to be said that wasn't already discussed?" Allen asked, showing no signs of distress.

"Please, come take a seat," Alejo said politely. Allen stared at Alejo then turned to his two sons and nodded his head as the three men walked back towards their chairs.

Alejo wasted no time and immediately began his over the top speech. "I was born in Mexico and raised by wolves. I was taught that you kill or be killed. When I rose to power by slaughtering my enemies and my friends, I felt no shame," Alejo stated, looking around at everyone sitting at the table. His son Damacio swallowed hard as his Adam's apple seemed to be throbbing out of his neck.

"As I got older and had my own family, I de-cided I didn't want that for my children. I want-ed them to understand the importance of loyalty, honor, and respect," Alejo said proudly, speaking with his thick Spanish accent, which was heavier than usual. He moved away from his chair and began to pace the floor as he spoke. "Without un-derstanding the meaning of being loyal, honoring, and respecting your family, you're worthless. Family forgives but some things are unforgivable so you have no place on this earth or in my family."

Then, without warning and before anyone had even noticed, blood was squirting from Felipe's slit throat. With the same precision and quickness, Alejo took his sharp pocketknife and slit Hector's throat too. Everyone was too stunned and taken aback to stutter a word.

Alejo wiped the blood off his pocketknife on the white shirt that a now dead Felipe was wearing. He kept wiping until the knife was clean. "That is what happens when you are disloyal. It will not be tolerated...ever." Alejo made direct contact with each of his family members at the round table before focusing on Allen. "I want to personally apologize to you and your sons. I do not condone what Felipe and Hector did and they have now paid the price with their lives."

"Apology accepted," Allen said.

"Yeah, now let's get the fuck outta here," Clayton whispered to his father as the three men stood in unison, not speaking another word until they were out the building.

"What type of shit was that?" Kasir mumbled.

"I told you that old man was fuckin' crazy,"

Clayton said shaking his head as they got into their waiting SUV.

"I think we all knew he was crazy just not that crazy. Alejo know he could've slit them boys' throats after we left," Allen huffed. "He just wanted us to see the fuckin' blood too and ruin our afternoon," he added before chuckling.

"I think it was more than just that," Clayton replied, looking out the tinted window as the driver pulled out the parking lot.

"Then what?" Kasir questioned.

"I think old man Alejo was trying to make a point, not only to his family members but to us too."

"You might be right, Clayton."

"I know I'm right. We need to keep all eyes on Alejo 'cause I don't trust him. He might've killed his crooked ass nephews to show good faith but trust me that man hates to ever be wrong about anything. What he did to his nephews is probably what he really wanted to do to us but he knew nobody would've left that building alive. The only truth Alejo spoke in there was he was raised by wolves," Clayton scoffed leaning back in the car seat.

All three men remained silent for the duration of the drive. Each pondering what had transpired in what was supposed to be a simple business meeting that turned into a double homicide. They also thought about the point Clayton said Alejo was trying to make. No one wanted that to be true as their business with the Hernandez family was a lucrative one for everyone involved. But for men like Alejo, sometimes pride held more value than the almighty dollar, which made him extremely dangerous.

Coming Soon

Sugar Babies...

A Titillating Tale

A Novelette

JOY DEJA KING

Read The Entire Bitch Series in This Order

P.O. Box 912
Collierville, TN 38027

A KING PRODUCTION

www.joydejaking.com
www.twitter.com/joydejaking

ORDER FORM

Name:

Address:

City/State:

Zip:

QUANTITY	TITLES	PRICE	TOTAL
	Bitch	$15.00	
	Bitch Reloaded	$15.00	
	The Bitch Is Back	$15.00	
	Queen Bitch	$15.00	
	Last Bitch Standing	$15.00	
	Superstar	$15.00	
	Ride Wit' Me	$12.00	
	Ride Wit' Me Part 2	$15.00	
	Stackin' Paper	$15.00	
	Trife Life To Lavish	$15.00	
	Trife Life To Lavish II	$15.00	
	Stackin' Paper II	$15.00	
	Rich or Famous	$15.00	
	Rich or Famous Part 2	$15.00	
	Rich or Famous Part 3	$15.00	
	Bitch A New Beginning	$15.00	
	Mafia Princess Part 1	$15.00	
	Mafia Princess Part 2	$15.00	
	Mafia Princess Part 3	$15.00	
	Mafia Princess Part 4	$15.00	
	Mafia Princess Part 5	$15.00	
	Boss Bitch	$15.00	
	Baller Bitches Vol. 1	$15.00	
	Baller Bitches Vol. 2	$15.00	
	Baller Bitches Vol. 3	$15.00	
	Bad Bitch	$15.00	
	Still The Baddest Bitch	$15.00	
	Power	$15.00	
	Power Part 2	$15.00	
	Drake	$15.00	
	Drake Part 2	$15.00	
	Female Hustler	$15.00	
	Female Hustler Part 2	$15.00	
	Female Hustler Part 3	$15.00	
	Female Hustler Part 4	$15.00	
	Female Hustler Part 5	$15.00	
	Female Hustler Part 6	$15.00	
	Princess Fever "Birthday Bash"	$6.00	
	Nico Carter The Men Of The Bitch Series	$15.00	
	Bitch The Beginning Of The End	$15.00	
	Supreme...Men Of The Bitch Series	$15.00	
	Bitch The Final Chapter	$15.00	
	Stackin' Paper III	$15.00	
	Men Of The Bitch Series And The Women Who Love Them	$15.00	
	Coke Like The 80s	$15.00	
	Baller Bitches The Reunion Vol. 4	$15.00	
	Stackin' Paper IV	$15.00	
	The Legacy	$15.00	
	Lovin' Thy Enemy	$15.00	
	Stackin' Paper V	$15.00	
	The Legacy Part 2	$15.00	
	Assassins - Episode 1	$11.00	
	Assassins - Episode 2	$11.00	
	Assassins - Episode 2	$11.00	
	Bitch Chronicles	$40.00	
	So Hood So Rich	$15.00	
	Stackin' Paper VI	$15.00	
	Female Hustler Part 7	$15.00	
	Toxic...	$6.00	
	Stackin' Paper VII	$15.00	

Shipping/Handling (Via Priority Mail) $8.95 1-3 Books, $16.25 4-7 Books. For 7 or more $21.50.
Total: $_____ FORMS OF ACCEPTED PAYMENTS: Certified or government issued checks and money Orders, all mail in orders take 5-7 Business days to be delivered

CPSIA information can be obtained
at www.ICGtesting.com
Printed in the USA
LVHW101247220822
726557LV00002B/71